Burr

BURR

Brooke Lockyer

Brooke Lockyer (signature)

NIGHTWOOD EDITIONS

2023

Nightwood Editions
P.O. Box 1779
Gibsons, BC VON 1V0
Canada
www.nightwoodeditions.com

COVER DESIGN: Angela Yen
TYPESETTING: Carleton Wilson

Canadä

Canada Council   Conseil des Arts
for the Arts   du Canada

BRITISH COLUMBIA   BRITISH
ARTS COUNCIL   COLUMBIA

Nightwood Editions acknowledges the support of
the Canada Council for the Arts, the Government of Canada,
and the Province of British Columbia through the BC Arts Council.

This book has been produced on 100% post-consumer recycled, ancient-forest-free paper,
processed chlorine-free and printed with vegetable-based dyes.

Printed and bound in Canada.

LIBRARY AND ARCHIVES CANADA CATALOGUING IN PUBLICATION

Title: Burr / Brooke Lockyer.
Names: Lockyer, Brooke, author.
Identifiers: Canadiana (print) 2022048841X | Canadiana (ebook) 20220488428 |
    ISBN 9780889714427 (softcover) | ISBN 9780889714434 (EPUB)
Classification: LCC PS8623.O32 B87 2023 | DDC C813/.6—dc23

In memory of my father.

PART ONE

Got a date to see a ghost by the name of Jones
Makes me feel happy to hear him rattle his bones
He's one man I always know just where to find
He's one man I always know just where to find
When you want true lovin', go and get the cemetery kind

—Sid Laney and Spencer Williams, "Cemetery Blues"
    (as sung by Bessie Smith)

Jane

I look for my father under my bed. I look inside laundry hampers, beneath the cushions of couches and chairs. I stick my fingers in the cold toes of his shoes. Sometimes I find something that smells of him. Other times a strand of his hair, shining silver when I hold it to the light.

I trace the cracks in his shrunken soap. I inspect his tweezers, squeeze his nail clippers open and closed. Brush the dry bristles of his toothbrush with my finger. Drag his razor over my thumb until it bleeds.

I enter my parents' bedroom when Mom isn't there. I sniff his side of the sheets. Check his white cotton pillowcase for eyelashes or scabs or dried pools of spit. Examine the shape of his pillow for the indent of his sleeping head.

I pull parking slips from his jacket pockets. A travel comb, loose change. I dig deeper, the tips of my nails darkening with lint.

I open his drawers and bury my face in his favourite flannel shirt. Press the socks he'd folded together in pairs. I thumb through the ties hanging from the rack, swaths of bees and trout waiting to be knotted around his neck.

I want to find a letter with my name on it. An envelope with his voice trapped inside. A conversation I can unfold with my hands.

I search all over the house though I know it's no good. My father thought he would live long enough to see me get married, have a child or two. Why would he have hidden a goodbye for me when I am thirteen and he forty-two?

I find other things I shouldn't. A prescription for a drug I can't pronounce. A curled photograph of a couple I don't recognize. The girl grins at the camera but the boy looks only at her, one hand covering a polka dot on her bikini. A letter from my mom with the words *Happy Birthday, Henry. Love, Meredith* in her blue cursive. A stack of mismatched greeting cards. I flip through them anxiously but find silence inside.

In the kitchen, I notice Dad's preliminary autopsy report tacked on the corkboard above the telephone, wedged between a New Orleans garden and a crossed-out to-do list.

I read it carefully, trying to glean clues from what the doctors discovered inside. Trying to understand why a heart "attacks." I place my palm over my heart and feel it beat. Will it turn against me too?

Dad's heart was the weight of four plums. *Within normal limits,* said the autopsy report. *450 grams.*

When they cut him open they found other things. *Congestion of lungs and kidneys. Simple renal cyst, left kidney, mid-pole.* I sit at the table and read the report again and again. Below his Adam's apple, a scarred, butterfly-shaped gland.

Each time I read it, Dad becomes less like himself. Each time, a little more dead.

Meredith

Meredith stands on the porch, gazing at the black maple in her front yard. In another month, the leaves will rust.

Flowers were unfurling when Henry dropped dead. It happened on their anniversary. They'd taken the afternoon off work. After the funeral, there was a heat spell that lasted for weeks. Sweat seeping through her hairline and the armpits of her shirts. Her daughter pulling away when reached for. (Or was it the reverse?)

She kneels and ties the laces of her running shoes into bows. Ever since her husband died, she's relied on long walks to cope.

Meredith doesn't realize how much she's missed the library until she sees it. She ducks under the familiar awning when it starts to rain, wanting to be close to her place of work but not inside. Through the small side window, she watches Mrs. Beatty, her boss, type and wonders if she made a mistake by taking a leave of absence. She misses the cart she pushed steadily through most of her adult life, the squeak of wheels on carpet accompanying her through singledom, marriage and motherhood.

She met her husband Henry in London, Ontario, when she was in her first year of university, struggling to cover tuition with shifts at Huron College library. He'd watched her over the top of *Fifth Business* five Wednesdays in a row as she strode past his chair. He barely turned a page when she was in sight.

She discovered later it was Henry who had hid books for her to discover. She uncovered *Dance of the Happy Shades* nestled with *Love Story* in her cubbyhole when she pulled out her scarf (how he snuck into the employees' room, she didn't know). In the shadowy corner of the Politics section, Meredith found *Lady Chatterley's Lover* and *Where the Wild Things Are* heaped on each other, pages shamelessly spread.

The same afternoon, after her supervisor left and they were finally alone, she wrote her number on his bookmark. When he said goodbye and turned to walk away, she pulled him to her, biting his lip when they kissed.

A few years later they got hitched and moved to Burr. Meredith worked weekdays at the small library there, while Henry commuted to his new job in London where he worked as a risk analyst.

Even though Henry no longer flirted with her in the library, she still loved finding misplaced tomes hiding in foreign territories, left there by the lazy and absent-minded. She'd ponder their significance, as if they were tarot cards or tea leaves.

Usually her findings were modest, her interpretations mildly life-affirming. *Feeling the Shoulder of the Lion* mistakenly slotted in Fiction, *Life Studies* left open on a ledge. But when she discovered *Invisible Man* and *The Sound and the Fury* leaning spine by spine against the side of a windowsill, an unexplained premonition spread through her body. A pervading chill, like when she was six years old and swallowed all the ice cubes in the tray.

Another time she found *Beloved* and *In Cold Blood* lying face down on a cobwebbed shelf. Thrilled and nervous, she crept to the phone to cradle Henry's voice against her ear.

On weekends, Meredith and Henry rocked in wooden chairs on their porch, dipping their knees and faces into the sun, awed by what they'd done, by the new life they'd begun. They took horseback riding lessons from their neighbour on Saturday afternoons, breathing in horsehair and leather, spurring flanks with their thighs.

On summer evenings, they walked through the countryside as the heat began to ebb, stepping around fox dens and catching fireflies, feeling the wings throb inside their hands for a moment before they let them go, to blink like tiny lanterns through the trees.

Ever since the library switched to a computerized system, it had been Meredith's job to beam the red light along barcodes as she checked out books for customers. Before reading the information that flashed on her computer screen, she would peek at the person across the counter and guess whether they read romance or crime novels, if they returned their books on time, and if not, whether they requested extensions or allowed the fees to accumulate. She was pleased when she was right, and also when she was wrong. She was happy when people surprised her. It was like finding a watermark in an old book, or deciphering marginalia on a page.

Henry had surprised her. The way he'd shed his gentleness in the change room and emerge a big stealthy cat in his wrestling singlet, eyes bright as he and his opponent circled around and around on the mat. Henry almost always pounced first, almost always won. From practice bouts at Huron College in London, Ontario, to the World Wrestling Championships in Toledo, Ohio, he'd crouched over dozens of surrendered bodies, shyly victorious, looking up to see her reaction.

She'd prop her head with an elbow while he slept, willing his parted mouth to disclose its secrets. The childhood in

Paris, Ontario, he refused to speak of, changing the subject and carefully turning away from her when she pressed. The family she'd never met. The reason he sometimes shouted in his sleep. Unfamiliar names that sounded Seussian, made-up. A diatribe about a man who lived in a shadow. Once, he pointed at her and claimed he saw a mountain lion in the trees.

The time she woke to him standing on the bed, pressing his hands against the ceiling and grinding his teeth, as if he were holding up the room, the whole house, as if everything might collapse the minute he let go.

Meredith dreamt during the day. When the books were organized and the library quiet, she'd sit at the checkout counter reading royal biographies. As she turned the pages, the ceiling rose into the sky and the faded carpet gave way to a floor inlaid with gold.

When she'd walk home afterwards, the houses on Main Street were dumpier than before, the hedges more disgruntled. She would dart from the library as if she were late, giving quick waves to the neighbours who turned their heads, methodically moistening their lips to talk.

Since Henry's death, people keep telling her to rest, but she feels nervous all the time. She no longer strides about town, spine straight, dress flirting. Lately, she hesitates, she questions, she shivers. She wears tights but her legs still tremble. (Unlike Henry who had crackled with heat. He wore T-shirts year-round and, in the dead of winter, opened all the windows of the house.)

She doesn't tell anyone how restlessly she sleeps. Instead, she goes over to Ruth's house for biscuits and tea, grateful her friend lets her pretend everything is fine. At home, she talks to her daughter Jane over defrosted dinners and curls up with the cat to watch period dramas. But Henry won't let her rest.

Meredith backs away from the window, into the rain. She doesn't want Mrs. Beatty to know she's there. She's almost reached home when she passes old Ernest Leopold, ambling by in the opposite direction. If he sees her, he doesn't let on.

He holds a cane with one hand, and a tattered black umbrella over his head with the other. Water streams through, pasting down his hair and soaking his pinstriped pyjamas. He's paler than the last time she saw him, his blue-white skin almost translucent.

Meredith crosses her arms over her chest and bows her wet head. She'll go back to the library next month and work shifts once Jane's back at school. She misses the paper cuts. She was secretly proud of those thin red lines, of their humble, manageable sting.

Ernest

The first time Ernest sailed into London's Meadowbrook Centre, he was only eighteen, cresting on visions and churning sheets.

The room was clean and white and smelled of vinegar. Orderlies swept dandruff and earwax under beds, although occasionally human debris found its way into dustpans and up the moustaches of vacuums.

There wasn't much to do in the hospital bed. Ernest dreamt when he slept. When he couldn't sleep, he focused on chewing and swallowing his food, and making as little sound as possible as he padded to the bathroom in his slippers. When there weren't meals or other bodily needs to attend to, he gazed at the water stain on the ceiling, imagining it was a cloud.

One afternoon, he amused himself by naming the constellations of freckles on his body after favourite musicians. Muddy Waters speckled his feet, while Howlin' Wolf dappled his hairy chest. Ernest opened the powder compact he'd borrowed from his mother's purse during a visit and inspected his face in the small round mirror. The butterscotch smattering on his nose was definitely a boogie-woogie John Lee Hooker. He stroked the powder puff with its pink bow before dozing off in his tightly tucked-in bed. Awake or dreaming, Ernest tried not to think of the half-finished notebook his mother had left for him, the one with his drawings of Evelyn and him together at the beach. He kept the salty pages closed, out of sight.

He saw the book sink slowly, his handwriting drifting off the pages in strings of black seaweed. He trembled when he saw his sister's palms splash the water before going under.

He hadn't done enough to save her. He hadn't done anything.

Watching from the shore, eleven years old, he'd been mesmerized by the gulls and the way the sun hit the water, how her screams disappeared just like that.

Burr

Unlike unassuming Paris, or the nearby village of Dublin, Burr lives up to its name. The prickly fruit is everywhere in this flat Southwestern Ontario town, clinging to socks and sleeves and hair. Dogs' tails wag low and heavy. Cats flatten their ears as they bite at the spikes caught in their fur, trying not to pierce their tongues.

As in all towns on the edge of wildness, nature intrudes in small and disruptive ways. Snails devour gardens, trailing slime. Residents pour beer into vats for snails to drown in or remove their shells and sauté them in butter if they're feeling cosmopolitan. "Escargots," they announce, sprinkling guests' plates with parsley and tucking Eiffel Tower cocktail napkins underneath. In Burr, everyone pronounces the *T* in escargot, even the ones who know better, not wanting to seem pretentious.

If you drove down Main Street with its mix of gingerbread-trimmed Victorians, bungalows, rambling farmhouses and simple storefronts, you might think there was nothing special about Burr, nothing much to differentiate it from the other villages and towns dotting the periphery of London, except that the people of Burr have chosen to live here. They are proud of this choice and keep scrupulous watch over everyone else seeking a quiet life.

The people of Burr believe it best not to speak of unseemly matters (although they gossip among themselves anyway, unable to help it). They try not to talk about that night in 1880 when a vigilante mob murdered a troublesome family with spades and picks and fire, dousing the homestead with oil and cheering as it burned.

"That's long gone," they say now if pressed, waving their hands dismissively. "It's a nice peaceful town."

In Burr, there's Oxbow Elementary School and Medway High School and St. John's church and Pete's Butcher Shop and Burr Food Mart and Deedee's Diner and the flour mill and Max's Variety and an Esso and a library and a cemetery where a young girl lies face down in the soil and dreams of being buried.

Jane

Annie is my best friend. We met three years ago, playing dead on the gymnasium floor. Our classmates sprawled around us, clutching their throats or lying belly-down like starfish. I preferred a simpler pose. Back pinned to the linoleum, knees touching, eyes closed. Annie, who had just moved here from Vancouver, lay on her side, a mosquito-bitten arm propping up her head. The game was Graveyard and we were starting fifth grade.

Miss Shoebottom dimmed the lights to set the mood. "Lie down, Annie," she ordered. After a few hushed moments, her heels clicked their way out of the gymnasium.

"Thank God," said a stage whisper to my right. A few minutes later: "Come on, let's hide on Shoebottom." I remained motionless, deciding a dead girl wouldn't listen to anyone, particularly not a new kid.

"She's doing this so she can have a smoke break," Annie insisted in a distinctly unghostlike voice.

"Shh," I said, finally.

"Shh," said the other fifth-grade corpses.

I wanted to imagine what it feels like to be dead. I wanted to think about Michael Jackson moonwalking in "Thriller" and the girl whose head was tied on with a ribbon. (Her lover wouldn't stop pestering about why she wore the ribbon so eventually the girl let him untie it and then her head fell off.) Graveyard was my favourite game and Annie was ruining the vibe.

"It's not even a real game," she whispered, tugging my sock.

I ignored her for the rest of the day but Annie still gave me a gap-toothed smile when they let us go. Something about her tall-girl slouch and the way her Converse shoes pointed inward won me over. I slowed to let her walk with me.

On weekends we played Orphans. Behind my house, we locked ourselves in the dog run with a box of matches, a bowl of blueberries and half a loaf of bread that wasn't stale enough.

We rubbed dirt on our cheeks. We sprinkled it on the berries. We tore our T-shirts. We rationed the food ("one for you, one for me") in the bowls we made by cupping our hands. We gave a couple of blueberries to the neighbour's old German shepherd but he nosed them until they rolled away, his tail thumping out a lonely beat.

We stomped to the forest and brought *Island of the Blue Dolphins* as our manual. The woods were dark and cool, trees blocking the sun. By the glow of Dad's flashlight, we read how to make lamps out of silver fish, fashion spear points from sea elephant teeth and build fences from the rib bones of whales. We dreamt of survival and sea salt, making do with candles, two silver-painted sticks and rows of curved branches stuck in the dirt.

We drew plans to construct a raft but couldn't find any logs. The trees in the forest were alive, so we climbed them instead, calling each other Nefertiti and King Tut, and later, Bonnie and Clyde. We took turns playing the man. I stole an eyeliner from Mom to thicken our eyebrows and draw sideburns curling from our ears. We plucked red clover petals and nibbled the sugary white ends.

It was my duty to rescue Annie from the daddy-long-legs that crawled up her body. I told her they were harmless but she'd shriek unless I removed them right away. You had to gently take hold of one of the spider's legs, otherwise it would come off along with the one on the opposite side of its body like a giant wriggling staple.

This summer, our bodies bled and the forest began to lose its magic. We pretended it wasn't happening at first, forced ourselves to jump and run and scream and climb as before, hiding our fear that the shaking limbs might break. The white pines and hemlocks thinned, Main Street now visible from our base at the foot of the creek.

We raided Mom's stash of *National Geographic* and brought our favourites with us. After reading about Amazon warriors, Annie said a stud was needed to ensure the future of the Orphans, our two-girl clan. The next day, we rode our bikes over to the baseball diamond. Andrew Milligan took off his shirt after the game. His nipples shone pink in the hazy sunlight. Annie pointed. "That one. Let's take him back with us."

There was something serious in the way she stared. My heart thudded. "The Amazons wouldn't choose him."

"Why?"

"I can't imagine him riding a horse. Besides, isn't he kind of short?"

She shouted, "Hey Andrew!" then twirled on her sneakers, grinning when he looked over.

She didn't notice Ernest Leopold following us around again. Didn't see him across the other side of the diamond with his camera, tilting his trilby hat at me.

She didn't see me lift my hair to show him the black plastic tattoo choker I wore around my neck, my tribute to the girl with the ribbon.

Meredith

Meredith wraps the blankets around her in a cocoon. The bed is too big, too cold. The alarm clock throws its heavy hands against the seconds in the dark.

She's waiting for Henry to come back from the bathroom, mouth minty with toothpaste. For a moment. Until she remembers. If she didn't have these moments anymore, Henry would truly be gone.

The cocoon is too tight, too constricting. She tears off the sheets and nightgown, throwing them away from her. She turns on the lamp and pulls on underwear, jeans, socks and a sweatshirt, and steps quietly past Jane's door. In the kitchen, she ties her feet into running shoes, grabs a flashlight and closes the door behind her.

The night reverberates with insects. She likes the way her footsteps sound against the chorus of hidden voices. Left, right, left, right. She follows the beam. She's not sure where she's going. It doesn't matter. She just goes.

As she walks, she sheds tension like a silvery husk. All around her, death's imminence—on the rustling spines of leaves and the wings of moths. She didn't hear this deathly frequency when Henry was alive, when they'd convinced themselves they were invincible. They were careful in enough ways. They never travelled at great speeds in cars, skied through trees, smeared butter on toast, ate bacon or sweets. They deserved death on their own terms, when they were ready, smiling softly in slumber, touching their wrinkled faces together in agreement.

But death was unpredictable. Why did they pretend otherwise?

For Henry, it was a terrifying and emasculating concept. But why had she, so macabre as a child, played along? Was she scared now too, particularly of the prospect of their only child left truly alone? Was it a fear of willing death into being by thinking it? An unwitting inheritance from her Christian Scientist grandmother, though Meredith could barely remember her, since the impossibly stoic lady had died fairly young of bone cancer?

Meredith shines her flashlight down the path, illuminating popcorn kernels and movie stubs. The wooden sign glows *Mustang Drive-In* when she lifts her beam. It's Saturday and the midnight feature is in its final half-hour. The woman at the booth is absorbed in nail filing and Meredith slips undetected through the gate.

She sits on the hill behind the rows of cars and gazes at the bodies in the back seats and the particles hovering between projector and screen. Meredith hugs her knees as the blonde on the screen is attacked by a masked, chainsaw-wielding man. The blonde screams silently as she's splattered with her own blood. The director zooms in on her crimson eyelashes and breasts, as if her destruction is sexy.

When they were newly married, Meredith and Henry would drive to the Mustang to make love in front of the flickering screen. They circled until they found a spot at the back, shaded by trees. When the sun dropped, they fumbled over her bra hooks, tracing their lips along necks and earlobes and nipples, hot breath fogging up the glass. A scene from a different kind of movie.

There were outtakes too. Meredith accidentally set off the windshield wipers or Henry's elbow hit the horn or they got tangled in seatbelts. They'd giggle as they crawled into the back seat, skin sticking to vinyl as they rocked, Henry whispering "Love you" down the nubs of her spine.

Afterwards, they got dressed and lay on the grass, barefoot and bruised. Meredith rested her head on Henry's chest, tucked her fingers under his. The dark deepened. They watched stars mouth their lines on the screen and listened to the voices tuning in.

Sometimes they stayed at the drive-in after everyone had left. Meredith would turn the car's radio dial until she found the Beatles and they'd press their cheeks together and slow dance where the other cars had been, feeling the tire tracks under their toes, stepping over plastic cups and ketchup packets. Cows stared at them from the other side of the fence, flicking their tails.

They'd keep dancing even as the song ended and the commercials came on, until the grizzled man who owned the place said, "Show's over, folks. Time to go home."

Meredith spots him now, shuffling out of his hut as the cars stream out of the field in single file. His back hunches as he moves, from decades of weekend shifts under the moon, picking the bits of garbage from the grass.

As Meredith walks home, the night lifts its black lace skirt. Is Jane sleeping, or did she wake up, sensing her mother was gone?

They've shared the sight of so many transformations lately. Henry at the funeral, his eyelids arranged to convey peacefulness, his powerful body stilled in the coffin. Meredith's own body shrinking daily beneath black clothes, hair sprouting silver.

As she follows the curve of the driveway to the door, Meredith thinks of her daughter's transformation, the T-shirts tightening around her breasts, the skinny limbs growing stronger. The banshee music floating out from under her door, her newfound silences, the way she smirks into her hair at nothing at all.

Jane

Ernest Leopold sleeps with the body of a young dead girl.

My best friend Annie tells me this as we spit pistachio shells into the creek in the late summer light. "Yeah, right," I say.

"It's true," says Annie.

"Why would he do that?"

"It's either an afterlife thing, or a long-lost love thing. I can't remember." She lowers her voice. "He carries a picture of her in the left pocket of his trousers wherever he goes."

"*Trousers?*" I arch an eyebrow. "Are you sure they aren't pantaloons?"

"His pants. Whatever."

We munch quietly for a moment, imagining Ernest's wrinkly face.

Almost nobody sees Ernest Leopold at night. Except for me. I've seen him. His rickety frame stoops in our vegetable garden. Bony fingers pull leafy plants to his face.

He comes by more now, since Dad died. Crouching in ragged pyjamas, eyes gleaming through the slats of our picket fence. Sometimes I lie on the front lawn to look at the stars when I'm missing Dad so much I can't sleep. Once, as I pushed the door open to go outside, I saw him. It was like he knew I would come down the stairs, he'd been waiting for me to appear. A flash of light burst from his lifted hands before he loped off, an ancient camera draped over his shoulder.

I didn't tell anyone about Ernest taking my picture, not even Annie. I'm not going to tell her now.

Dad used to sneak up and take my picture too. Or take it from far away, zooming in his lens as I read under the apple tree or waited for Annie. When I opened the Kodak envelopes he brought home from the city, I blushed when I discovered the secret way he saw me, the soft hang of my face when I thought I was alone.

Ernest

Ernest wondered if Meadowbrook was helping him. Despite the daily rhythm of meals, therapy, exercise, free time and sleep, he found it hard to keep track of how much time was passing.

At night, he dreamt of twins in lace dresses. They blew dandelions into thunderclouds and when they shook their heads, rain fell from their hair.

He dreamt of his dead sister too. She stood on a beach, said, "Give me your hand," and placed a pearl in the knot of his palm. He folded his fingers over it carefully. *Evelyn.* She crawled into a shell when he called her name.

In the morning, in his hospital bed, he awoke with sand between his toes. Pebbles skimmed over doorways and closets. His mouth tasted of seaweed.

Swan-necked nurses bobbed around his body, combing his hair into a nest. At lunchtime, they fed him peas and boneless chicken. A can of apple juice with a pink straw.

"What do you see?" the psychiatrist asked him in the afternoon, holding up an ink-blotted page.

"A ship," Ernest said. The man blinked through round lenses. "A fisherman's net." He didn't tell the doctor about the hole in the net, the one that let all the trout swim away, shimmying their speckled backs off the page.

His mother came to visit him, bringing flowers and a new fountain pen. She cried and buried her face in his skinny chest.

Her tears felt nice through his cotton gown. He said, "Thank you," and patted her head until she left. The room shifted and lurched. If she came again, he didn't remember.

There were times he coasted alone on waves of darkness. A month where he stopped speaking. He spent his days listening to the constant lapping of footsteps, of pills washing smoothly over his tongue. He felt his mind unspooling within him, casting him adrift in the bleach-rubbed space.

Jane

I'm not ready to go back to school. But Annie is.

My bedroom is a total mess. Clothes strewn everywhere. Nothing fits. I don't want to start eighth grade tomorrow. I don't want to be the girl everyone still whispers about. Hopefully by now, pity over my dad is dead.

I walk into his closet, braving the loud ticking clock and fusty smell. Were the mothballs always there or did Mom recently put them in his drawers so his sweaters and socks will last forever? I run my fingers through Dad's ties, lingering on the country scenes, the ones with the fish and ducks and horses he wore the most. I gaze at the family photographs on his dresser, our smiles mostly genuine beneath the glass.

After a while, I open the suitcase in the middle of the floor, still packed from his last business trip. I pull out the items— yellow toothbrush, sheepskin slippers, grey pyjamas, razor and shaving gel, a pair of wool socks, Hanes underwear, a white-collared shirt that smells of him—and lay them in a row. After I've memorized each one, I put them back, the way they were, in his suitcase. I zip it closed, turn the little baggage lock before pocketing the key and carefully closing the door.

Back in my own bedroom, I take last year's class photo down from my wall and sit cross-legged on my unmade bed. Annie's proud that we're pretty much the only girls not wearing Beaver Canoe sweatshirts. I'm in a Hypercolor shirt, hair half hiding my face, neon pink shooting from my armpits. Annie, in a vintage Blondie tee and boot-cut jeans, stares down the camera.

When Annie told me back in fifth grade that she was from Vancouver, I wasn't surprised. She wasn't like anyone I'd ever met before. The morning she strode into our portable classroom, I could smell the ocean on her, a salty West Coast glamour. She was teenaged at ten years old, always the tallest kid in class. Her calves were muscular, probably from climbing so many mountains.

She spoke of sushi restaurants, eels slithering in the tanks, the male chefs with shiny ponytails. She knew how to crack open lobster claws, how to suck the meat from the legs. How to order dim sum. How to eat fish heads, eyeballs and all. The other kids thought she was a show-off but I listened carefully to every word she said.

She told me when I met her that she'd only be in Burr for a year or so before her mom got restless. We could still be friends, she said, she just wanted me to know. They only came to Burr because that's where her mom had grown up and her granny was losing her mind.

I used to worry she'd leave me. Now I'm both relieved and disappointed her family might be stuck in Burr for eternity too.

Annie says it's hard being here after Vancouver. No volcanoes anywhere, not even a mountain, the flat landscape going on forever.

Annie's brother Dylan is four years older and looks nothing like his mom or sister. Annie says it's a shame he hasn't made any hot farm friends he can bring over for us to torture, leaping through the backyard sprinkler in my one-piece faded rainbow Speedo and her new black string bikini.

Before Vancouver, they'd been in Nanaimo, where the dessert bars came from. Before that, some place Annie called "the Interior" where she was pretty sure her dad still lived. Annie shrugged, but her face was flushed, uncertain. He was finding himself, she said.

Annie's mom wears flowery dresses and has loose, waist-length auburn hair. She's had a lot of boyfriends, Annie says, and the last one was a real dick. Now Paula tells her kids she's learning to be alone.

Their house looks the same as the other brown-brick houses with beige siding on her block but it's interesting inside. A living room we aren't supposed to enter, where all the furniture is covered in plastic. "For company," Annie said when she gave me the grand tour, rolling her eyes.

"Not that we ever entertain," Paula chimed in with a delicate laugh.

Under the resigned watch of three Virgin Marys, Annie and I clambered on the couch that day, tickling each other and smothering our giggles on the weird-smelling vinyl, thrilled that Granny could come in anytime and catch us. I loved the awful way the plastic stuck to our sweaty legs and mouths, protecting the cream fabric and its dainty strawberries.

Annie said Granny likes me because I'm a kindred spirit. I asked her what she meant and she said I'm basically an old lady trapped in a thirteen-year-old body. I hit Annie with a pillow and she laughed and said she wasn't joking. I smelled like lilacs and used too many big words. I asked her why I was her best friend then, and she said there weren't too many options, before sweetly kissing my cheek.

Annie has a vocabulary as big as mine, she just chooses not to use it in public. When we swap books, hers are spicier. Raising my R.L. Stines for Christopher Pikes, my Judy Blumes for V.C. Andrews.

I try on a plain black sweater with a pair of faded flares and comb my dirty-blonde hair into a centre part. Annie will probably think I look boring, but I want to disappear into the crowd. I turn to see my silhouette in the mirror, standing up straight for once instead of hiding my new curves in a slouch.

I'll grow into my nose, Mom says. My mouth is big too, my eyebrows what she calls "strong."

Meredith

Meredith's walk leads her through the outskirts of Burr, into the forest's mouth.

The ground is soft. She removes her socks and shoes, relishing the way her feet sink into the earth. Sun filters through the trees, making delicate patterns on the ground. A beetle traverses the sock lines imprinted on her ankle.

The air washes Meredith's lungs and rib cage in a cool pine scent. The trees scrub her clean. Her fingers unclench and her toes spread deeper into the dirt. *Shinrin-yoku*, the Japanese call it. Forest bathing.

She finds some logs lying side by side, knotted with vines. Through Meredith's dreamy eyes, they become a raft in the dappled light. She strokes the logs, perplexed. Did her husband do this, knowing she'd come? She drags the raft behind her, but after a few steps it falls apart. *Get your head out of the clouds*, she reprimands herself. *Not everything has to do with Henry.*

Meredith ventures farther from the forest path and discovers something strange: a bed in the middle of a thicket. A proper bed, with a curved wooden headboard, two plump pillows, a ruffled skirt and a quilted bedspread tucked under the mattress, the corners perfectly folded.

She creeps closer. It's relatively clean and dry, barely touched by falling leaves, rain or animal paws. It can't have been there long, maybe a day or two.

How the hell did it get here?

She steps back into the shade, waiting for footsteps, voices, some sort of clue to explain the bed's existence.

But the woods are quiet apart from the rustling leaves and the odd burst of birdsong.

There were easier places to dump a bed if the previous owner had grown tired of it. And even if the bed had been ditched, why would it be made up so nicely? If someone had brought it here to hide out in the woods, then where were the rest of their possessions?

As the sky bruises its skin, an idea slowly takes shape. Could Henry have brought it here? She takes off her shoes and tests the corner of the bed with her foot and the mattress springs back, like a real, normal mattress. "Crazy," she mutters. But was it much nuttier than the other explanations she'd thought of?

She lifts the quilt and fingers the clean sheets. They smell of cinnamon and sandalwood. They smell, inexplicably, of Henry. A squirrel stares, clutching a nut between his toes. She looks to see if anyone else is watching before slipping onto the sighing bed. She pulls the Henry-scented sheet over her nose, breathing him in deeply, her hand darting instinctively under her skirt, breath coming quicker and quicker until she shudders and the stars jump into focus.

She puts on her shoes and makes the bed. As she leaves the forest, she glances over her shoulder to make sure it's still there.

The next day she comes back with a large bag, nervous the bed will be gone without a trace. But when she enters the secret thicket, it's there, just as she discovered it the day before, covered with a thin layer of leaves and dirt. She brushes it off and gasps when a squirrel pops out of a pillowcase. Is it the same squirrel from yesterday? She likes to think so. She laughs as he flaunts his fluffy tail before scampering up the trunk of a tree.

As the squirrel races from one tree limb to another, she's glad there's no rational explanation for the bed. It returns the world to the way it was when she was a child. Somehow, it also brings her closer to Henry. She hangs a photograph of him that used to live in her bedroom on the branch of a tree. Next, she pulls slippers out of her bag and tucks them under the bed.

She crawls under the quilt and looks up at the shifting clouds. When the rain starts to fall, something bursts inside her.

Am I losing my grip?

The rain streaks her cheeks. Streams down the framed photograph hanging from the tree.

She pictures the rain falling on Henry's cheeks, Henry's lips, Henry's chest. She imagines the rain washing him up out of the earth in the middle of the thicket, like a jellyfish on a beach after a storm.

Jane

Annie and I walk to school together like we do every year, scuffing our sneakers along the pockmarked road, Annie talking about how she wishes we were anywhere but here, me trying not to think about Dad.

There's not much to do in Burr, except hitch rides to Mason-ville Mall and watch reruns of *My So-Called Life*. Annie and I wouldn't be caught dead in those sweaters with moose or kitten designs stitched into them. No babies at sixteen, no livestock classes at 4-H, no drugs in the back of Randy Wayne's pickup. We shake on it, solemnly.

We're going to start a band and move to New York City. I'll be Johnny to her Joey Ramone. At least, that's what Annie says. Personally, I think I could be Siouxsie Sioux, wailing about the happy house that never rains. Annie can chop off her hair and thump away on Budgie's drum kit.

Either way we need to get out of here fast, before it's too late. Burr seizes you by its prickly mouth when you're not paying attention. Look at the adults; they walk around half-dead most of the time, wearing old-fashioned clothes and chanting "time for bed" and "true love waits" from their white faces. No one in Burr believes too much in Buddha or poetry or punk or any of those things the rockers in *Rolling Stone* believe in. (No one even knows what *Rolling Stone* is. We have to get Annie's brother to smuggle it in from the city for us.)

There's only one thing everyone in Burr believes in: Ernest Leopold. All the kids say something about him.

He eats only green food and paints with his toes. He can do both feet at the same time.

He collects lost children.

Rare bats breed in his basement.

He has cats (thirteen) and a pet raccoon.

"You don't really believe Ernest Leopold sleeps with a dead body," I whisper to Annie.

"I've heard it from a couple of reputable sources."

We're sitting at the back of Mr. Matthews' math class. He swings his long arms back and forth as he explains the semester's geometry assignments. I cover my notebook in triangles, picture Ernest spooning a skeleton, braiding a ghost's flowing white hair. Annie draws the teacher, then scribbles him into a monkey, before carving *Nick Cave* into her desk with a Swiss Army knife. The room is hot and the teacher's voice goes on and on.

I prop up my head with an elbow. Dad is dead and I'll never be with him again. What's the point of learning the Pythagorean theorem?

I tear a page out of my notebook and write, *Skip with me?*

We pretend we have to go to the bathroom, then sneak out. As soon as we're outside, I feel better. I race Annie to the creek and almost beat her.

"What will your lover be like?" Annie asks.

"Mmm. He has to like swimming and be a good dancer. And have dark eyes. What about your lover?"

"Me, I'm going to have lots. They have to smell good and not be too skinny. I wouldn't kiss all of them though."

"That would be gross."

"Yeah."

"Wanna go swimming?"

We strip down to our underwear and jump in, then scramble out for front dives and back ones, cannonballs, pikes. When we're tired, we lie on a grassy knoll.

"Let's practise kissing," Annie says suddenly.

I sit up.

"We have to be ready for when it happens for real," she says, averting her eyes and crossing her arms over her goose-pimpled chest. Annie pushes wet hair out of her face then places her hand at the nape of my neck, shoving her face toward mine. We bump noses. Annie doesn't laugh. I don't either. She tries again, closing her eyes and angling her head to the side this time, freckles zooming in.

I place my hands around her waist, trying to maintain some space between our bodies. Heat radiates through her skin.

I tell myself it's not really a first kiss. That it doesn't mean anything.

When she tries to French, I imagine it's doll-lashed Sunrise Records Noah I'm kissing. The curve of her hips messes with my fantasy and I'm worried something is changing between us and I can't shake the feeling of a slug crawling into my mouth. I push her off and she wipes her lips with the back of her hand.

We cannonball into the deepest part of the creek, shaking the reflection of trees and shattering the sun into pieces. Underwater, our bodies are green, hair twisting around us like seaweed. Fish fins slip against our kicking legs. I come up for air and Annie makes faces at me. I'm laughing until something moves in the grass behind us. Annie turns slowly, following my gaze.

Ernest Leopold.

He's dressed in a black suit and tie instead of his usual pyjamas, wispy hair gelled stiffly off his forehead. Annie stares at him but he ignores her. He stoops to place something in the grass before he ambles off, the wind flapping his coattails. A figure from an old photograph come to life.

We pull on our clothes and run to where he stood. Hidden in the grass, a thick, heavy brown envelope with *Jane* scrawled on the cover. "Open it," Annie says, her sparkly nails tearing at the paper.

I hold it out of reach. "Not now."

"Give it," she says.

"No."

Annie's face crumples. I watch her swinging ponytail as she takes off, not sure why I'm not running after her.

I walk home slowly, hugging Ernest's gift to my chest.

Mom's making dinner. I place the package carefully under my bed, saving it for when I'm alone and there's less risk of her walking in on me. I tell myself the payoff will be better, like having to wait until Christmas to find out what's under the wrapping paper.

As I stand up, Ernest's coattails rustle in my ears. I shiver, the creek dripping off the ends of my hair.

I open the fridge. A defrosting pot pie from a neighbour, a platter of sausage rolls, cubed cheese. I spike a marbled square and chew slowly. The house is strange with so many cut flowers. People keep bringing them, even though it's been over four months now. I wish all the flowers would get it over with and die.

Groucho leaps onto the kitchen table, blinking his green marble eyes, then rubbing his black head against my body and purring. I turn and stare at his tickling whiskers, missing the way Dad's eyelashes would brush my cheek when he read me a story. Remembering the hardness of his belly as I sat on his knee, the sound of his thumbs slowly turning the pages.

I wanted the scary ones. Bluebeard was my favourite, with his forbidden room and curious young wife. Before I went to bed, I would crouch inside Dad's bear arms as he read, skin prickling as I waited for the bloodied floor, the lovely dead girls hung in a row. His breath blew warmly against my cheek as he told me about the key no scrubbing could wash clean, the blood that wouldn't wash away. The narrow escape.

If I could, I'd dig myself into the ground to be with him. I'd brush off all the bugs and dirt from his nice blue suit, rub his smiling face clean with my fingers.

While I'm setting the table Mom comes into the kitchen and asks me how the first day back at school went. I shrug and concentrate on folding the napkins and putting the cutlery in the proper places. If she notices my wet hair, she doesn't mention it. We eat, our forks poking chunks of chicken and carrots as they slide out of the steaming pastry on rivulets of gravy.

The fan whirs in circles as I wait in bed for Mom to fall asleep on the other side of the wall. She's into big books lately, the ones featuring multiple generations of families, passionate lives spanning continents and centuries.

Mom never caused a scandal, but she used to be bold. Men would turn their heads as she moved through a party. She had that kind of walk. She was fun too, a bright blur of laughter that spun around me as I tried to cling to her nylon knee. I hid under her skirt when I was little, dodging the points of her high heels.

It was actually Mom I was closest to before Dad died. Mom, who I worshipped and wanted to be. She knew about witch trials and Mongolian eagle hunters and some village where a guy would kill a goat in your honour and you'd eat the whole beast together, slurping on head soup, scooping marrow from hooves. She tickled my toes to wake me for school and brought home ghost stories for me, books on Arctic expeditions for Dad, making us laugh with her imitations of head librarian Mrs. Beatty and her lectures on the dangers of slap bracelets and the books of Christopher Pike.

Dad called Mom a space cadet because she was constantly misplacing her keys. She could travel somewhere far away when she was with us, but never for long. In those moments she was a star, twinkling remotely from outer space.

I made fun of Dad to bring Mom back to earth. He was the least goth person ever. He wore ties with barnyard animals on them. He read books on the power of positive thinking. He framed his diplomas, displayed his trophies on a shelf. He chose movies where the good guys always won. (Unlike the ones Mom preferred, which were tragic or mysterious or both. A servant girl cuts open a papaya and boom: pregnant.)

Now Mom wears faraway looks and low pumps that hesitate in the doorway. I close my eyes when she takes off her shoes and tiptoes into my room. She creeps closer and sits on the edge of my bed. She strokes my hair even though she knows I hate it when she touches me now. I wonder if she can smell the creek on me. After a while, the bed creaks and her footsteps recede into the heart of our house.

After she's gone, I reach under the bed for the package and turn on my flashlight. Under the brown paper is a diary with a green leather cover and gold-edged pages. Between them, a red leaf crumbles along its spine, a cluster of starflowers smear their yellow stamens. I turn the pages.

A folded sheet of newspaper with my father's obituary circled in red. A sheet of music with notes pencilled in. A black and white photograph, overexposed. I'm standing in the doorway of my house in my nightgown, an apparition with tangled hair, pressing my palms against the door.

Meredith

Meredith stood with her daughter to face the receiving line that shuffled toward them, smoothing her long black dress. There were wreaths of daisies and baby's breath, and the sage-green chapel ceiling was covered in a pox of pot lights. The room felt fake, like a funeral home TV set.

"I'm sorry for your loss," people said. The refrain of condolence struck her as odd. As if they had taken him away from her. As if they were the reason he was dead.

Meredith racked her brain for her lines, feeling utterly miscast. "Thank you. And thank you for coming."

"You're handling this so well," murmured the wife of Henry's boss.

Was she? She blinked at the elegant woman from her dry face.

After peering in the casket, Henry's former wrestling coach circled back. "He looks so alive," the old man marvelled. "Like he could get up and dance."

Meredith grasped her daughter's hand stiffly while Jane smothered a nervous laugh.

Henry had requested an open casket in his will. Meredith couldn't fathom why. Surely, it was the least natural thing you could choose. His neck injected with formaldehyde that spread through the arteries of his body, pushing blood out his jugular vein. Organs punctured and drained. His mouth filled with cotton then sutured shut. Henry's corpse growing firm and rosy. Even in death, a robustness. A simulated healthy glow.

Meredith stole a look at the funeral director who'd embalmed him. She should have been the last one to touch Henry intimately. Not him.

Why couldn't she have prepared his body? She was overcome with jealous desire. She imagined it was she who closed his blue eyes. Released rigor mortis by flexing his limbs and fingers. Positioned his hands one on top of the other. Soaped and massaged his body. Covered his genitals. Combed his hair. Shaved his face before moisturizing with light pats of cream.

Meredith refused to be arranged by a stranger and put on display when she died. She preferred to burn in a furnace set to eight hundred degrees Celsius. An urn on her daughter's mantle filled with five pounds of bone dust.

Jane

Dad had smelled funny in the funeral parlour. He'd been dead for almost a week. His hair was stiff and didn't move when I blew on it when no one was looking. I touched the fine down on his cheek, touched his freckled hand.

When they put the man who wasn't my father in the ground, people wept. I kept waiting for my real dad to appear, his brown shoes tapping up the path.

I was startled when Ernest Leopold came up to me with some wildflowers held together with string. He said my name as he gave them to me. People stared but he didn't mind. He stood a couple of paces to my right as they covered the box with dirt. For some reason I was glad he was there. Annie kept glancing at me and blinking. I could tell she was trying not to cry and I wished she would pull herself together. She thought we had something important in common now, but her dad was alive somewhere.

At the reception, later, someone gave me an hors d'oeuvre, saying it was important to eat in times like these. I stared at the shrimp beached on my napkin, wishing it would swim away.

I knew Dad was dead, but I kept seeing him alive. I scanned the reception and found him broken into pieces and thrown about the room. I spotted his salt-and-pepper hair perched on another man's head, his confident stride setting a stranger's body into motion, his quick smile on unfamiliar lips.

Sometimes, when I'm about to fall asleep, I imagine his coffin is under my bed. When I open the lid tonight, Ernest is there instead, in his black suit and tie. His beard glints blue in the moonlight. He beckons me closer and I crawl inside, clutching the scrapbook he gave me and closing the top so no one will find us. We lie together in our wood-panelled home and he clasps his hands around me in the dark. He whistles a tune between his loosened teeth. He whispers to me and the sea rushes into my mouth.

Burr

When Henry and Meredith Blackburn moved to Burr, the locals were watchful at first, waiting to see what kind of people the young married couple from London would turn out to be.

There was pride there, and defiance. An assumption that people from bigger places (or those who did white-collar work in them) looked down on locals. But it was the urbanites who were the ignorant ones, lacking basic survival skills. Most couldn't milk a cow or grow their own food or read the weather.

Standing in their Italian leather boots, the city people passed judgment on the unsentimental way the locals treated their farm animals. Tricked by cute cartoons and storybook creatures, they didn't understand the natural cruelty of the animal world. Meanwhile their Siamese cats roamed the fields leased to real farmers, mass-murdering the birds.

The young Burrs were smart. They won ribbons showing horses and heifers in 4-H, and could ace the school tests too, even though some were pulled out of school for stretches at a time to help with the crops.

When Arthur Leopold was running the brewery and his estate, he employed loyal kids at his summer soirees. They sweated in rented suits as they held out trays of canapés. Students from the University of Western Ontario music department were hired to drown out the crickets and frogs with upbeat jazz. Ernest was sometimes seen at an upstairs window, pressing his ear against the screen.

Burr still had a bit of glamour, if you knew where to find it. There were the Gordons, producing generation after generation of figure skating champions, and Jack Amber, a cardiac surgeon who bred rare Egyptian Arabian horses. "Drinkers of the wind," the silver fox would quote to his audience of Hollywood stars and rich investors, before his multi-million-dollar business was incinerated in scandal.

The Arabians were the oldest purebreds in the world. The same breed depicted on ancient tombs, the same horses that carried Napoleon and Washington into battle. The surgeon thought about his horses all the time, even while performing triple bypass surgery. He loved their high tail carriage and floating trots. He was fascinated by their insides. Per pound of horse, Arabians have much greater heart and lung capacity, he would marvel, than any other breed.

There was an amateur rodeo scene too, with real Albertan flavour. The fans hollered in their cowboy hats and Garth Brooks T-shirts, excited by the whiff of danger in the air. Barrel racers running their horses in cloverleaf patterns and steer wrestlers wrangling horned beasts to the ground.

Meredith

Meredith sits cross-legged on her forest bed in the dimming light. She shoos a few glittering beetles off the leaf-strewn covers. She puts on her dead husband's sweater and switches on her flashlight when she can no longer see.

She lures a moth with her beam. Inspects the dead wasp she finds on the bird-stained bedspread, illuminating the once-venomous body and delicate wings. Shines a light on the portraits of Henry and their family.

Meredith and her husband believed life was simpler a hundred years ago, when folks were more in tune with the land. Henry in particular took this romantic notion to heart. Henry, who wore sunscreen reluctantly and who, for minor ailments, chose unpasteurized honey from his hives as his go-to medicine.

Shortly after moving to Burr, Henry hired someone to dig a pond behind the house. He let everyone assume that the pond was there naturally, and the largemouth bass too.

He bought a child's rod for Jane once she was old enough and taught her how to cast a line and reel it in. They stood side by side in the tall grass, heads tilted at the same angle as the sun beat down on their khaki fishermen hats.

In the beginning, they kept what they caught. Henry gutted the fish in the kitchen sink. Jane held on to the edge of the island, fascinated by the flash of scales in her father's hands. Meredith would ask her daughter if she felt like a snack, but no matter what she offered—an apple, a cheese string, raisins in a box—she was ignored. Jane focused completely on her father, on the quick, unsentimental way he deboned and descaled the fish, saving the silvery green heads for the cat.

The barbecue had a small handprint spread over the grill bars. Jane had made odd dares for herself, like "cross the room in five giant steps!" and, one fateful day, "touch the barbecue... or else!" Meredith knew that in her daughter's fervent imagination, these dares possessed unmentionable consequences if she failed.

Jane's blistered hand had healed quickly but the memory of her silent scream lingered, and Meredith noticed that her husband stared at the spot where the handprint had been each time he heated the grills.

He'd brush the fish with President's Choice teriyaki sauce or a homemade paste of butter and dill and lemon, but no matter how he dressed them, the fish were coarse and tasted of the pellets that supplemented their pond diet of algae, weeds, leeches and worms. Henry was hurt when Meredith complained.

"Like kibble," she'd whispered, crinkling her nose, when Henry's back was turned and her daughter had asked how "pellet fish" tasted. Jane didn't like fish no matter what they were fed, and it wasn't fun grilling only for himself, so Henry eventually switched to catch-and-release. When city friends came by, they'd leisurely have a go, casting their line into the pastoral fantasy he'd cultivated, hoping for a tug.

She knew it was ridiculous (they had a microwave and a TV and a car after all), but Meredith pretended the pond was natural too, and treasured its unruly elements most. There was green slime and a white rowboat with a hole in the bottom and mosquitoes that swarmed over the stagnant water. There were snapping turtles that would swallow your toes if you'd let them. There were frogs and toads and, in the beginning, two geese that could almost pass for swans.

The geese had been given to Henry and Meredith shortly after they'd moved to the country, as a sort of pond-warming gift. It was said they mated for life, and it's true that when the female was killed by the neighbours' dog years later, the male disappeared shortly thereafter. "Died of heartbreak," Meredith told anyone who inquired after the missing goose. "Probably in the woods."

Jane clung to her mother as she recounted the story. "It's so romantic," she'd chime in with a sigh.

Meredith turns the dead wasp in her hands and smiles. Jane had inherited her own fascination with the macabre. At eight, her daughter folded origami headstones and beds for the stiff and ailing flies she found around the house, which she then lined up in her cemetery-slash-hospital shoebox. She persisted, despite Henry's efforts to convince her that houseflies were germ-infested, but she did don a pair of faux-silk gloves from the costume trunk as a concession.

Meredith suspected that her husband wasn't sure what to make of his little girl, who had no interest in sports and dressed up as a bat, swooping down banisters, arms outstretched. Once, when Henry reached into the closet for his coat, he discovered her fake-sleeping on her head, wings ceremoniously folded against her chest. She bared her fangs when he jumped.

On Saturdays, as Henry pushed her through the supermarket in the cart, she'd repeat things like "spaghetti" and "donkey" until the everyday words became strange.

"We may have a budding poet," Meredith told him brightly in the tuna-can aisle, trying to alleviate the concern in his face as their nine-year-old daughter played with the syllables in her mouth.

Henry did understand Jane and Annie's orphan games. Like his daughter, Henry fantasized that he was a survivalist living off the land; he didn't mind that the whole conceit relied on Jane imagining her parents dead.

In summer, the grasshoppers rubbed their legs and the bees buzzed and the garden grew tall and lush. The tomato plants towered over their stakes, the fruit weighing heavily on their hairy green stems. Meredith's husband plucked each one as if it were a gleaming ruby. ·

"This was growing in the garden ten minutes ago!" he'd crow.

Meredith would laugh at Henry's outsized enthusiasm. But it was true. The tomatoes tasted of sun and earth.

After watching *Fried Green Tomatoes* on TV with Jane, they began battering the tomatoes in flour and frying them before they were ripe. They'd slice them in Western sandwiches and slip them in burgers or eat them fresh. Jane liked the way the salt drew out the tang but when she asked her father to pass the shaker he'd lift his eyebrows and say, "The white poison?" and Jane, unfazed, would roll her eyes and say, "Pass the white poison, Dad."

Meredith had found this exchange amusing at the time. Why would he bedevil the salt shaker? There were bigger things to be afraid of.

There was also the time she put a cheap blood pressure cuff in his Christmas stocking to tease him for being vigilant about his health. He put it on one arm, then the other. He made her do it, then Jane, but grabbed it back when their numbers were lower than his. He turned it on and off. Removed the battery and put it back in. They laughed at his determination to beat the cheap thing. It was broken, they were sure of it. Not him.

Her husband never said anything was wrong when he came back from a doctor's appointment, but that was part of his wrestler's code. Courage to Henry meant fighting each battle mano-a-mano. Courage was mind over body. Courage was coughing in the back kitchen where no one could hear you and denying having a cold at all costs. Courage was confronting challenges with a positive attitude and a heap of backyard honey on a spoon.

"Isn't Mother Nature great?" Henry would say, rubbing Meredith's back as they drank antioxidant-rich red wine by the pond after Jane had gone to bed. (She wasn't really sleeping, Meredith suspected, but reading Roald Dahl paperbacks under her sheets by flashlight.)

Meredith put her arm around his waist as the frogs croaked in the dark. Secretly, she felt melancholic about the fish swimming round and round. Did they know it was all a simulacrum and they were truly dependent? Did they care, as they vacuumed pellets down hook-scarred throats?

She wanted to ask her husband again about his childhood. To hear how his older brother had tricked him up a silo when he was eight and left him there, laughing from below as Henry peed himself in terror. The anecdote had slipped out in the car, a sudden tightness in his face warning her not to ask more.

But she needed to know what he was afraid of, what he worked so hard to suppress. What kept her from knowing the people who had raised him. What wound him up.

Why couldn't he trust her? How could she truly know him if the most formative chapter of his life was ripped out of the book?

She tried catching him in different moods, tried asking in different ways. "Let's talk about something nice," he would say.

Sometimes, when Meredith was ironing Henry's shirts, or meeting with the Oxbow bake sale committee, or scooping turds out of Groucho's litter box, she felt oddly panicked as she pictured the bass swimming below the surface.

On her way back to the house, the stars are smaller than usual. A million holes pricked with safety pins.

Ernest

After his sister drowned, Ernest couldn't bear to be home with his parents and Evelyn's ironed dresses and white socks. He hid in the apple tree in the backyard and wrote her name on paper planes he sailed into the dark.

When he was a teenager, he wandered the streets of Burr, looking for signs of his dead sister. At the variety store, he plucked her favourite candies from glass jars until the paper bag couldn't hold any more. He went to the schoolyard after the kids had gone home and played hopscotch where she used to play hopscotch and ate a gummy worm and tried not to think of her pearly teeth chewing candy and her small pink tongue.

When they released him from Meadowbrook the first time, he was nineteen. He decided to live on the streets of London for a while, rather than face his father again. The first night he curled up on a bench in the park. In the morning, he found a weeping willow to sit under. He leaned against the trunk, poking his feet out from under the stringy green hair.

He made friends with a cat with a patchy coat and mismatched eyes. She hissed and purred at the same time, kneading his sweater until it fuzzed. Her sandpaper tongue chafed his skin.

Days passed. He forgot to count them. The cat ambled off and didn't come back.

One day he saw a girl wearing Evelyn's shoes. He trailed the shoes with his eyes until he couldn't see them anymore, then got up and followed them on his stilt legs. The shoes stopped after a few steps. He reached out his hand and she took it. "Look," the girl said.

His face was dirty and his eyes were wet. He had a hole in his trousers. But his hand was warm and his smile familiar.

"Come," he said.

When the parents found their daughter, she was asleep in his lap on the bench. They trembled as they pulled her limp body away.

"She's fine, but…" the girl's parents whispered. As the girl with Evelyn's shoes slept soundly in her bed, the whisper spread beyond London's borders. Burr grew suspicious too.

Ernest was afraid of getting beat up on the street. He was relieved when he was committed again. Winter was coming and Evelyn wouldn't leave him alone. Back in the hospital, he found people treated him coldly. Now the doctor asked him what he thought of little girls, a bit of gravel grinding his voice.

Meredith

When Meredith was a child growing up in London, she had a cat named Esmeralda and a dog named Boris. One morning, while stirring cream into her coffee, Meredith's mom noticed the cat lying dead on the kitchen floor. Boris, their elderly border collie, was curled around the corpse, his black and white legs trotting after phantom bunnies. Meredith's mom spilled coffee on her slippers, murmured, "Jesus Christ." She fetched her husband and they buried Esmeralda in the backyard before Boris and Meredith woke up.

Later that day, while Meredith was drawing pictures of Esmeralda and splattering the crayoned paper with tears, Boris dug up the dead cat from the backyard grave and carried her gently in his mouth to the door, scratching with one paw to come in. When Meredith opened the door, she backed away screaming—Esmeralda's head and legs poked stiffly from Boris' jaws. She ran and hid in the closet while the dog came inside, squeezing her hands over her ears to shut out the sound of Boris' panting and Esmeralda's rigor-mortis limbs tapping on the closet door.

Meredith's dad tried to retrieve Esmeralda from the clamp of Boris' jaws by dangling toys, and even a ham bone, but Boris would not let go. In the middle of the night, Meredith's parents crept to the kitchen while Boris was asleep and carefully pried Esmeralda from the dog's paws. Meredith's mom held the flashlight while her husband shovelled in a different spot, deeper this time.

Meredith's dad placed rocks on top of the cat's grave but Boris dug around them to get to Esmeralda. Meredith's dad hid Esmeralda in a new grave behind a shrub, but during the annual garden party Boris sniffed out the dead cat and lifted her from the earth, drooling. He trotted with her triumphantly into the circle of guests.

"It's Esmeralda," a neighbour said grimly.

Red velvet cake slid off a paper plate and a couple of punch tumblers shattered as they hit the ground. Someone tittered. Conversations were abandoned. The guests made excuses, begged off.

While Meredith's parents plucked forks and broken glass from the lawn, Meredith hid behind a tree. She peered around its bark to watch Boris play with Esmeralda on the porch, batting at her playfully with his paws and propping her against the wall with his nose, licking what was left of her face.

Meredith felt guilty for being afraid of Esmeralda, especially next to Boris' unwavering devotion. After all, it wasn't Esmeralda's fault that she was dead, that her fur was matted and missing in some places, that her moon bones were showing through. "Sorry, Esmeralda," she whispered desperately into the bark as she wept and pinched her nose.

Meredith's parents had wanted to keep Esmeralda in their backyard for their daughter's sake, so she could plant poppies and offer prayers. They thought it was important for Meredith to learn how to show respect for the dead.

But it was impossible. Everyone had been horrified by Esmeralda's resurrection at the party and the trio of little open graves in the yard. They would no doubt remain wary of Boris too, misunderstanding his loyalty, suspecting he'd dug up Esmeralda to finish off what was left of her remains.

The next morning, Meredith's dad laid the dead cat on a blanket in the car and quickly rolled the windows down. Boris poked his muzzle inside, whining as Meredith slipped into the back seat and somberly elbowed him out.

They reached the woods as dusk was settling. The ground bore the tracks of foxes or wolves, and as they buried Esmeralda's fur-tufted skeleton, Meredith sensed eyes in the trees. The cat was sticky with rot and Boris' saliva when Meredith placed her, for the last time, in the grave.

She gagged as the dirt wriggled with worms, and covered her wild, wet face with her hands. Her father was silent as he shovelled some loose soil on top.

Jane

Salesmen knock on our door sometimes and ask where my dad is. They want to speak to him. The man of the house.

Usually they're selling God and salvation. Jehovah's Witnesses with fervent faces and ill-fitting suits pressing doomsday pamphlets into my hands.

This morning while Mom is still sleeping, it's a Conservative Party campaigner with an acne-scarred face.

I dig my jagged fingernails into my palms and say, "He's not here." We have a conversation about when he might be back, how he might be reached and what he does for a living.

I'm only partly punishing him for being nosy and too sexist to ask for Mom.

Eventually I say Dad is underground and the campaigner's eyes widen, picturing Dad as a political dissident in a foreign land or a miner with coal-smudged cheeks.

"Like, in the dirt," I elaborate.

"A gardener?" he asks, confused.

I imagine my father turning from green to blue to grey. Coffin flies laying eggs in his body, his abdomen blooming with mushrooms, golden moths feasting on his hair. His body seeping through the casket. The soil around him darkening, becoming nutrient-rich.

"Kind of," I say.

The steak man came by once too, his van filled with different cuts of meat. Dad bought some T-bones from him last year but they were too tough to chew. I looked him in the eye and told him Mom was resting and my father was dead. I kept my tone even, matter-of-fact. But it didn't matter. Like everyone else, he attempted to comfort me, recalling something he read on a Hallmark condolence card rack.

He's watching over me. He's in my heart.

I imagine my heart with Dad shrunk inside of it. Was he running his hands along the chamber walls as we spoke? Feeling the ventricles for signs of vulnerability, double-checking the valves? Scouring plaque from my arteries, breathing into my blood?

The steak man said Dad's spirit will always be with me. But sometimes I don't know where he is. Sometimes I don't feel him at all.

In one hundred years his bones will have turned to dust. There will just be his teeth and some grave wax. The waistband of his briefs, the nylon seams of his argyle socks.

Meredith

Meredith stood near the kitchen window in her sailor dress, waiting for her mother to finish drying the dishes and leave the room. Three days had passed since she'd buried Esmeralda in the woods. On the other side of the pane, Boris lay gloomily in the sunshine, head resting on paws. Later, she'd go outside and wrap her arms around him.

The house was awful without Esmeralda. Her absence roared. White noise rushed to fill in the space. Now the water pipes clanged, the fridge groaned and the appliances buzzed at high frequencies, hurting Meredith's head. She strained her ears for the soft ba-dumps of Esmeralda's landings on countertops and window ledges. Deep down, she knew the house had also lost Esmeralda, and with her, its usual rhythms.

Meredith ached for her cat. Could she sacrifice her crayons or her fairy-tale collection, for one last kiss?

She'd read in a library book that in certain cultures, human sacrifices could get you what you wanted. But who to sacrifice? A classmate? A friend? She'd feel guilty, especially if the kid shared his snacks with her at recess and didn't deserve to die.

"You do what you gotta do," her father was fond of saying— but could Meredith do it? Could she toss another child into the volcano or a witch's cauldron, or wherever the best sacrifice places were these days?

She imagined she could. After her schoolmate was incinerated or ladled into a bowl of stew or whatnot, Meredith would get Esmeralda back for a farewell lick and the momentary act of evil would be worth it. She'd press her face into Esmeralda's rumbling fur and tickle Esmeralda's pink paw pads and double-blink when Esmeralda double-blinked and stroke under her chin until the hot scratch of tongue was bestowed on Meredith's nose.

Boris yelped outside. Maybe if she threw in an extra third grader, the volcano goddess or witch would grant him a few moments with Esmeralda too.

"Penny for your thoughts?" Meredith's mother asked.

Meredith blushed. She focused on cold, impenetrable thoughts. Icebergs drifting for centuries. Snowdrifts in doorways trapping people in their homes for days. Her parents' tight-lipped fights. Hard-packed snowballs. Moby Dick.

Her mother had an uncanny ability to read her mind and didn't usually need to pay a penny.

"Not a good enough trade, huh?" Meredith's mother said tenderly. "Well, we could make cookies after I finish the laundry. Would you like that, Merry?"

"Mmm," Meredith managed, breathing easier.

As soon as her mother left, Meredith got on all fours and crouched in front of Esmeralda's food dish and ate some kibble that no one had the heart to throw out. She lapped water from Esmeralda's goblet. She ran her mouth delicately along the glass rim. Esmeralda's germs vibrated on her lips.

Meredith arched her back. Mewed.

She was dismayed to learn Southern Ontario didn't have any ordinary volcanoes, let alone ones with wish-granting goddesses.

"Why?" Her mother stirred the cookie batter, bemused.

"No reason." She threw in the walnuts.

That left witches. But you couldn't ask your parents where the witches were. They appeared when you least expected it, even though you had prayed for them for days with all your might. It was supposed to be a surprise when the witches actually showed up, their black hats poking out of the mist. They usually came at twilight, Meredith knew from books and TV, when you were alone and feeling very, very low.

Meredith was feeling very, very low. On the school bus, she stared at the houses with the most haunted reputations: the derelict Gothic with the sneering gargoyles and crumbling turret. The stone cottage possessed by a maleficent ghost. The black brick house where the blind woman with the wart on her nose lived. It was difficult to know where the real witches lived. Which broomsticks were for sweeping and which were for flying. Which ovens were for baking cookies and which were for burning lost children to a crisp.

Before Meredith went to sleep, she'd arc her body around Esmeralda's fur print on the bed sheet. She'd begged her mother not to launder it. She squeezed her eyes, remembering how Esmeralda's head would go up and down, up and down, as she measured the distance from the floor to the bed.

Meredith had nightmares. She dreamt of a rat wearing a ruffled clown collar. He performed backflips, showing off. He grinned with yellow teeth before taking a bow.

She woke with a jumping heart and the realization that all the bad things Esmeralda had scrupulously kept out could now tiptoe in.

Ba-dump, beat her heart. Ba-dump, ba-dump.

The witches never showed up, but Esmeralda did come back, in a way. When Meredith helped her mother take the hot clothes out of the dryer, they discovered Esmeralda's fur balled up in the lint tray. Later, as Meredith paced back and forth on the living room carpet practising her presentation on Ancient Egyptians, one of Esmeralda's claws snagged Meredith's toe.

Meredith stuffed the claw into an empty tic-tac-toe container along with the tuft of fur, and placed the box under her pillow—as evidence of Esmeralda's gradual resurrection, or for future cloning possibilities, Meredith didn't know.

The next morning, as Meredith poured milk for her cereal, a black hair floated down the white stream. Meredith slurped it up. She gagged but forced it down.

Everyone knew if you swallowed a cherry pit, a cherry tree would grow inside you. Was this a seed too, and if so, would the Esmeralda hair multiply inside her, would her heart grow fur? She chewed anxiously, unsure if she wanted to turn animal inside.

That evening, Meredith discovered Esmeralda sleeping on her favourite chair. The next morning, stretched out on the window ledge, watching the hummingbirds.

You couldn't look straight at Esmeralda, or she'd turn herself back into a shadow or a sweater and the lonesomeness would knock you in your gut.

You had to look for Esmeralda out of the corners of your eyes. Or when you were tired and your eyelids hung low. Then, maybe, you could see her.

A whiskered reflection in the windowpane. Phantom paws that raced along the floor before transforming into dappled light.

Ernest

Ernest spent his youth in and out of hospital, then in his late thirties, he suddenly found he had rights. He could live on his own, so long as he remembered to turn off the stovetop. Didn't hurt himself or anyone else. Deinstitutionalization of the mentally ill had become mainstream.

Sometimes, in a blue spell, he committed himself. Other times he burnt the blue onto paper. Made cyanotypes. He found a sun print kit at a garage sale, with instructions on how to do it. He wandered down country roads, looking for interesting shapes. A small carrot he pulled from a garden, with straggly roots and feathery green hair. Conjoined maple keys, the stained glass of a dead cicada wing. In the dark of his cellar, he arranged them on the page before bringing them into the light.

He made pinhole cameras out of his dead mother's shoeboxes. He stared through the hole at the upside-down world.

After he read a book on black and white photography, he converted his parents' bathroom into a darkroom, tearing down the shower curtain and blocking off the seams of the door with tape. He liked donning gloves and preparing the trays with chemicals in the red light. He liked the timers and cylinders and tongs. There was a scientific exactitude that was lacking in other parts of his life. (He'd failed most subjects at school but had liked biology best.) He bathed the negatives in the developer until what he'd captured seeped through the white.

The chemicals gave him headaches, so he hadn't replaced them when they ran out. Now he had to develop his photos like everybody else.

He hated the mall. The escalators put him in a stupor. He felt exposed by the bright lighting. Mocked by the teens in their uniforms with their knowing glances and chants of "Have a nice day!"

Jane

I should be walking to school with Annie but I don't want to. After the campaigner leaves, I decide to play hooky for one more day.

When Dad was alive, we rode our bicycles down the dusty roads fringing Burr. Bugs flew in our mouths and up our noses and we laughed deliriously but the wind snatched out the sound. We passed dogs straining on leashes and golden haystacks as our toes traced circles in the wind.

I take my bike out now and retread our familiar routes, pretend Dad is cycling beside me, turning his head to say, "My girl." Then I imagine it's Ernest Leopold pedalling next to me instead, leaning over the handlebars in his pyjamas, cheekbones poking out of his face. I crane my neck at my favourite barn as the birds flap their wings above my head.

The barn is actually only a splintering frame. If Dad and I timed it right, the sunset would stream through the chewed-up hole as we pedalled by, turning our faces neon.

We liked biking in inclement weather. We liked white puffs of breath. We liked the tears the cold dealt us. We liked the ragged eyeholes of our balaclavas. We liked the wet yarn stretched over our cheeks.

In winter, we pumped our knees past the Marshmans' place, where small lights hung over the frozen pond, illuminating the boys playing hockey furiously below. The game was an excuse for them to push and steal and hit each other with sticks. They hid their violence under puffy snowsuits and gloves and I imagined pinning one of their goose-feathered bodies under mine.

Race you. Race you to the top.

The last time we raced we crossed the peak of the hill nearly in line. As we flew downhill, we stuck our feet out from the pedals, letting gravity take us down. We grinned as the wheels spun and the wind smeared everything rushing by. I closed my eyes at the last moment, letting the darkness bring me down.

I ditch my bike by the apple tree in our front yard and start to run. I run like I'm being chased. I run even though I hate it. I'm not meant to move like that anymore. I'm not used to my changing body. This is how I'll die too, I think, my breath coming in too fast through the balaclava mouth hole, my ankles threatening to twist.

Which is what I secretly like about running. To keep going when I'm sure I can't take another step. To push myself through to another state.

I'm running along the road's edge when Ernest slows beside me in his car and offers me a ride. It's cold. Maybe he just wants to be nice. I'm following the route my parents took, the one they'd been running the day Dad died. I'm approaching the very spot. I shake my head at Ernest through the car window, my heaving mouth smoking up his face.

Mom never warned me about Ernest. Just strangers in general. "Don't get in the car," she says. "Even if they threaten you. Scream and kick and bite and fight. Once they get you in the car, you might as well be dead."

Where would Ernest have taken me? If he asks again, I might say yes.

Burr

In Burr, everyone knows practically everything about everybody. They know about Ernest Leopold's intermittent visits to
Meadowbrook Centre and the young girl who fell asleep in his
lap. They know about his sister.

At the service the town wasn't invited to, there was no child-
sized casket. Evelyn's body was never dredged, despite the
search team's efforts.

The family's money pushed people away. Their strangeness
too. No one left casseroles on Ernest's porch when he was suddenly the last Leopold left.

And now, with the house dilapidated, it would be risky to
make a house call. Who knows when the rotted porch would
give in or what wild creature could greet you from the rafters.
After years of isolation, how could Ernest be mentally sound
now, how could he possibly be safe?

They look away when he saunters down alleyways, whistling and winking his way into the sun. They pull their sons and
daughters into the folds of their skirts, banging small noses
against elbows and knees.

What they don't know, they will do their best to find out.

They don't know about Jane Blackburn and her fascination
with Ernest Leopold's deep-sown sorrow and rambling grace.
And they don't know how Ernest feels about Jane, the girl who's
lost her father.

Meredith

She tells herself she just needs a little more time. She tells herself that soon, she'll be ready to go back to work.

She sits by Henry's pond after breakfast, hands pulling at grass. She watches, unseen, as Jane rides off on her bicycle in the direction opposite to school, blue and white handlebar streamers flying.

"I'm not sure Jane's coming to school today," Meredith says apologetically when Annie shows up at the front fence.

"Is she sick?"

"Just having trouble getting back into the rhythm of things. I'll tell her you came."

Annie nods slowly and walks away.

How can she tell Jane not to skip school when she isn't able to return to normal life either? Meredith heads inside.

She pulls a book on William H. Mumler from the bookshelf, checked out before Henry died, now months overdue. *Each day brings its incidental fees*, she thinks, relieved penalties are being filed against her.

She's glad the mathematical evidence exists in the library database, that her withdrawal from her responsibilities is traceable, numerical even. Something she can pay back later.

William H. Mumler: divine spirit photographer or nineteenth-century American fraudster, depending on your point of view. Meredith was dubious of his claims when she read the book, but now she chooses to trust in him, chooses to believe he could expose the spirits of the dead with his lens. She's surprised by how eager she is to join the faithful, by how easily she can let go of her skepticism when she needs to. She wants to treat his photographs as empirical evidence that the deceased were there all along, comforting the ones left living.

The spine cracks as she opens the book to inspect the photographs. She traces the pale hovering bodies with her finger. The ghost of Abe Lincoln looking down in sorrow, his translucent fingers on his widow's shoulders, his dead son beside him, a boy-shaped glow in the corner.

She flips the pages backwards and discovers a bearded man named Robert Bonner, the silhouette of his dead wife pointing up at the sky with one hand, the other seeping through the lapel of her husband's black suit.

Meredith closes the book. She goes downstairs and rifles through a trunk filled with moth-nibbled blankets, Scrabble letters, broken crayons and Chinese checkers until she finds Henry's Polaroid camera. She licks a finger and cleans the dust off the lens.

She takes a picture of herself and sets it on her lap. Will her face emerge under the Polaroid's skin? Will Henry's?

A grim smile darkens the print before the rest of her face rushes in. She's reminded of the Cheshire Cat in his tree. The background is awash with light. It's probably the lamp behind her. But then again...

"Henry?" Meredith whispers.

She'll take a picture of herself outdoors in the natural light. Then she'll know for sure it's him. Meredith puts the book and camera in her purse and heads toward their forest bedroom. She startles a constellation of starlings when she enters the clearing and they circle over the suits Meredith hung from the trees two nights past.

She lies on the bed on top of Henry's folded sweaters and takes pictures of herself. She sits and crosses her legs, adopting poses from the book. She tries various angles, different shooting distances. She lays the Polaroids in rows at the foot of the bed over Henry's pinstriped shirts, her features coming into focus.

She waits for Henry to appear. Wonders if the curved branch in the background is an arm reaching out to embrace her. If the dot of a faraway plane is really the pupil of his left eye, watching over her.

Meredith tosses the last Polaroid. The ambiguous smears and spots have disappeared. Fully exposed, the photographs reveal her alone among the trees.

Jane

No one aside from Annie noticed I skipped school again yesterday. Either that or they've gone soft. Mrs. Thompson, the principal, offers me sad smiles whenever she passes me in the hall. She was the one who told me about Dad.

We were in English class and Miss Williamson was talking about poems and how they didn't have to rhyme when the principal knocked on the door and called my name. "Ooooh," sang my classmates. Mrs. Thompson gave them a look. I followed the principal into her office and sat across from her, waiting while she inched her bum to the chair's edge and spun her mug slowly, three times in a circle. There were brown rings inside it and a floating island where the cream had curdled.

Mrs. Thompson told me my dad was in the hospital and I felt small and cold in her office, swallowed up by the wooden chair with its clawed feet, a dingy string of light coming through the window. He'd had a heart attack.

I smiled, showing my teeth. "People have heart attacks all the time," I informed her. "Mother Teresa's had two." Mrs. Thompson pushed her glasses up her nose. "I'm sure he's fine," I said.

She patted my shoulder and told me Ruth would be picking me up any minute and how about a hug. I said, "That's okay, Mrs. Thompson."

In the car, Ruth chain-smoked cigarettes out the window.

"I basically quit," she said. "Just once in a while."

Her silver bangles clanged as she turned onto Main Street. She looked like she was about to cry. "He didn't make it, honey."

The house was empty when we got there. Mom was still at the hospital, tying up loose ends. Ruth wanted to wait with me but I told her I needed to be alone.

I crawled into my parents' bed, pulling the sheet over my head. When Mom came home, she crawled into the bed with me too. I pressed myself against her body, careful not to disrupt the impression of Dad's body on the mattress. The lamp shone warmly through the cotton. I pretended we were lying in a tent, camping out under the moon.

We pressed our wet faces together and she stroked my hair and told me stories about Dad in bursts, repeating the same ones over and over. It was nice knowing what came next.

She rubbed my scalp and told me how I used to escape from my crib in the middle of the night and fall asleep mid-crawl on my way to their bedroom. How I'd say, "Sorry, I'm all out of kisses," when Dad asked for a peck on the cheek. About when they were young and how Gran would flicker the lights from the top of the stairs when Dad was about to kiss Mom goodbye after he walked her home from the library. About his big freckled hands. She hugged her knees under the bed-sheet tent. They were supposed to grow old together.

I started stories too, saying, "Remember when..." and "Dad used to..." but I couldn't finish the sentences.

When Mom fell asleep with her mouth open, I shook her but she didn't wake up. I pressed my fingers to her wrist until I found her pulse, steady and warm in there.

Ernest

Ernest disappeared once.

He was at his sixth extended stay at the Meadowbrook Centre when it happened. His fingers vanished first, over dinner. He speared three peas before his fork clattered to the floor. He didn't remember letting go. When he opened his mouth to apologize, he found his tongue and lips had left him too. He stood and realized he couldn't see his legs or his toes. By the time he reached the end of the corridor he was sure no one could see him at all. He drifted behind the watchman pulling out his cigarettes and followed him out the hospital doors.

Ernest floated to a nearby park, pausing under a spindly tree. His heart twirled. He hadn't lost that. He counted the stars and listened to the crickets rub their legs together in the dark. He reached downtown London when day broke and fell asleep on Richmond Street, the pumps of secretaries and loafers of men strolling through him like he wasn't there. A goth wearing a black Victorian dress stood where Ernest's body ought to be and powdered her face.

He peered into the windows of coffee shops and record stores and bakeries and libraries and hardware stores and restaurants and clothing shops. He floated around snooty ladies and their little dogs. They tangled their leashes, barking wildly into the bright air.

By the late afternoon, he was sick of the city, of its rotten garbage and hurried heels. He slipped into the passenger seat of a convertible heading north. The silver-haired driver hummed along to "Mercy Mercy Me," gloved hands guiding the car from paved streets to gravel roads as dusk settled all around them. When she turned onto Main Street, Ernest rose from his seat and flew to the ground.

He drifted through Burr's backyards and gardens, passing through swing sets and barbecues, rose bushes and rhubarb. He felt lonely. He missed his body and he missed being seen.

Behind a white-slatted two-storey house at 71 Main, a young black-eyed girl pressed her nose against her bedroom window and stared at him. It would take him a couple of weeks to learn her name. Ernest gasped, felt his body return to him with a heavy, knock-kneed thud.

After a moment, Jane turned from the pane. He stayed in her garden, sniffing the vegetables with their glistening skins as hunger gnawed at his stomach. Next time, he'd return with his camera, feed her image gently through its teeth. He put a tomato in one pocket and a turnip in the other before heading off to the ramshackle estate that hadn't always felt like a home.

Jane

After school let out for summer, I sat at our usual booth at Deedee's Diner and ordered chicken fingers, fries and a strawberry milkshake for me; wiener schnitzel and a tomato juice (no ice) for Dad. It was the first time I'd been back since he died.

"Big appetite you have," Deedee said. I looked away when she smiled.

I didn't come here for Deedee to be nice. She'd never been nice in all the years we'd come during Mom's evening shifts, couldn't wait for us to leave from the moment we came in. Dad and I appreciated her grumpiness. It was as much a part of the experience as the splintering chairs and buzzing Labatt Blue sign.

I wanted Deedee's eyes to glare at me like before, an unlit cigarette dangling from the corner of her thin lips. I hoped she'd bring the wrong kind of milkshake and forget the ketchup, slam the plates down so the schnitzel jumped and the plum sauce splattered.

I pushed my coins into the jukebox and chose every song from *The Very Best of Cat Stevens*. I scowled as Deedee placed the food gently on the table, the milkshake perfectly pink. I stared at the door and waited for Dad to come in, ignoring the growls of my belly and the scent of plum sauce wafting up my nose. I swung my legs against the booth until our food grew cold and

Deedee said, "Jane, honey, we're closing up. You have to go after 'Hard Headed Woman.'"

I alternated spoonfuls from Dad's plate and mine, gulping down the food with tomato juice. I opened the door and walked into the sun, my stomach bursting with the meal I'd eaten for both of us.

July felt endless. I watched Clint Eastwood movies and drank all of Dad's beer, yelling "Pow! Pow!" as I galloped down the hallway, my fingers pistols. I didn't care if Mom heard me while she cooked or sorted the laundry. I was untouchable, the girl with no name. I burped my way down the stairs to the cellar where I hid the empties behind cardboard boxes and my cobwebbed baby stroller. (Except for the can with the lip-glossed rim that I left on Dad's desk, hoping my bad behaviour would raise concern, spark a resurrection.)

I spoke to Dad's doctor, dentist and barber, asked questions about the last time they saw him, took notes. I was seeking X-rays, scientific facts and a lock of his hair.

They told me what a kind man he was and how much they missed him. The barber said, "Only the good die young," but Dad and I aren't into Billy Joel.

I looked for Dad in the mirror but other than my square jaw, my reflection looked like me.

I wrestled Annie in my bedroom even though she was bigger, locking her in holds Dad taught me. I didn't release her right away. Sometimes I hurt her a bit.

Her dad might be a deadbeat but he wasn't actually dead. I dug my fingernails into her shoulder blades until she cried out. I left white fingermarks around her wrists.

I checked the mailbox three times a day, flipping through the condolence cards for a letter addressed to me in Dad's left-handed scrawl.

I wrote down a list of his distinguishing features:

1. *Really strong arms (can throw a thirteen-year-old girl up in the air, no problem).*
2. *Eyes the colour of my favourite blue jeans.*
3. *Laughs at his own jokes but in a contagious way so it's mostly okay.*
4. *Knuckles that rub my head with the right amount of friction.*
5. *His hugs. He pulled me tight the last time I saw him, whispering, "My girl," in my hair.*

Meredith

Ruth surfs topics between puffs on her cigarette, her voice brighter than usual. She discusses the best roadside stops for peaches, the War of 1812, and the dearth of naturally aging Hollywood actresses.

Meredith grips the edges of her chair. The chair's legs have teeth marks in them, from some previous owner's long-dead dog. When Ruth's eyes look into hers, Meredith returns her gaze. Why bother with the small talk? Can't you see I'm grieving?

At least it's a weekday. Friday, Ruth's regular day off from Fanshawe Pioneer Village. Meredith dreads the weekend. She's unsettled overhearing Jane talk to herself. Like her father, shouting out in her sleep. It's unbearable when they're together. The controlled politeness. The empty seat at the table. The raw grief in her daughter's face. Meredith tells herself that even if she tried to get close now, tried to recreate those first shocked days and nights together, she would only be pushed away.

She focuses her eyes on the surly wooden sailors standing sentinel behind Ruth's face—each wrinkle a nick of someone's knife. Above them, a quartet of blonde girls wearing white dresses and ruffled socks gazes at her from their pastel world. Ruth must have picked it up recently at some garage sale. Meredith has never seen the picture before. Ruth's always had terrible taste.

"Jerry says it's deliberate, not cutting the lawn. He calls it a bee and butterfly sanctuary—can you believe it? Is he a hippie or something? The sixties are over, okay."

Meredith raises her eyebrows but her friend witters on, oblivious. Ruth of all people, with her Laura Secord memorabilia and her work as a historical re-enactor, should understand the appeal of living in the past. She approves of Ruth's neighbour too. Why stop there, Jerry? Let it all go!

She thinks of photos she's seen from the Chernobyl alienation zone, of trees growing in abandoned classrooms and grasses growing from the busted hoods of cars. Of swans paddling in radioactive cooling ponds and lynxes cavorting near ruined reactors. Sure, everything was contaminated, but the animals' lives appeared joyful without humans. A small dose of radioactive cesium seemed a cheap price to pay for all that freedom.

"Meredith, are you listening?"

She nods, imagining bison roaming through Burr Food Mart and wild horses bedding down in two-car garages. She envisions albino wolves curled in Burr's bathtubs and two-headed black storks nesting in kitchen sinks. Cataract-eyed badgers hibernating under goose-down duvets and stunted minks dozing inside the pockets of grandmotherly fur coats.

She embellishes, winding the banisters in glow-in-the-dark ivy, adding trefoil-patterned wallpaper and chandeliers of radiotrophic black mushrooms. She'd coin the look "Cherno." Meredith: interior designer for the end of the world.

Jane

Annie comes over after school to check out the mail-order Rider-Waite tarot cards and garage-sale Ouija board I blew my allowance on. As I prepare to read her future, a gust of wind comes through the window and carries a few cards away. I rummage through my room trying to find them.

"It won't work now," Annie says, when I've given up and start to shuffle the incomplete deck. She applies my blackberry lipstick and pouts in the mirror. "You gotta have the full pack."

We set up a Ouija board séance on my bed, toasting to the dead with two goblets of Schweppes raspberry ginger ale. I grin at Annie and she grins back. We count down from three and close our eyes. My fingertips vibrate on the heart-shaped planchette.

After a while, I open my eye a crack. The planchette hasn't moved.

Annie stifles a yawn.

Dad, I say in my head, calm and reasonable. It's me, Jane. I'm here in my room. Waiting for you.

Time ticks by. I peek again, though I know the pointer hasn't budged. Dad. Are you there?

I lean forward as the planchette glides hesitantly to B and O and R. As it picks up speed, zooming to E, then making a quick swerve to D, I feel sick.

I throw the plastic pointer at Annie.

"What?" she says. "You don't really believe this stuff, do you?"

"You didn't even try to take it seriously."

"I'm sorry, okay? I'll make it up to you." She opens the curtains. "It's depressing in here. Like a funeral home."

"Get out."

"Shit. You know what I mean. Let's forget all this. Go to the park."

"Is Andrew playing baseball there?"

"It doesn't matter. I want to go with you. I want to be with you."

I ignore her as she keeps pleading, hating her. Finally, she leaves without me.

I sit at the Ouija board without her, fingers on the planchette, waiting for the dead to play with me.

I still check the mailbox every morning. I still turn on all the lights in the middle of the night so Dad can find his way back to me.

I dream of him and dream of him. I dream he's knocking on my door. I wake up in his nightshirt, shouting, "Come in!"

Sometimes the dream doesn't end with Dad knocking on my bedroom door. I'll walk downstairs in my pyjamas and there he'll be, sitting at the head of the table, as if nothing happened, smiling at me. I'm so happy, I can't believe it. But I don't know how to tell him he's dead. He's dressed for work, wearing his favourite herringbone vest, his brown leather briefcase leaning against the chair. I don't know how to explain that his office is empty, that he should just stay home with me.

I clamber into his lap, digging my fingernails into my fists. He strokes my hair, bewildered. He asks what's wrong.

Ernest

Ernest sits at the old upright piano in his ripped pyjamas, composing melodies in minor keys. His right foot presses the damper pedal gently, blending the notes into a legato. He wasn't allowed lessons when he was young. "Waste of money," his father Arthur had grumbled.

Arthur ran the brewery that had been in his family for generations. He had trouble relaxing outside the office and was secretly nicknamed "the Caesar" by the staff at the London tennis club for demanding new menus, reorganizing the patio layout and attempting to fire tennis pros over whom he had no authority. He was the type of man who expected to be greeted upon his arrival home by a Scotch on the rocks, the aroma of roast beef wafting from the oven and reverent silence. He was therefore peeved to return one day to lukewarm leftovers and his wife's entreaties for their son, who stood, scared and hopeful, in the corner.

Ernest was awed when his mother Edith bequeathed him her piano in her will. An act of rebellion from the other side of the grave.

Ernest had played the piano secretly as a child whenever he was in the house alone. His mother knew, of course, finding her sheet music in disarray, but never said anything, just smiled as she polished the silver. One time she left a book lying on the piano bench entitled *Music Composition for Beginners.*

That day Ernest taught himself how to shape silences into twisting leaves and how to turn music into dancing centipede legs. He spent hours arranging them on the slats of the fence. "Staff," his mother murmured dreamily as she drifted by, rubbing a tarnished platter. Mostly though, he felt out the music with his fingers. He hummed, eyes half-closed.

It's been ages since he's touched those keys. Only recently have the rhythms and melodies started playing in his ears again. The piano tuner hasn't visited in years and the notes turn sour as they rise from the hammers, curdling the melody. A few keys stick, leaking gaps into his homespun nocturnes, his honky-tonk ballads. He plays on and on, losing himself in the music as he thinks of Jane's bare shoulders surfacing from the creek. A moment before, the water had closed over her head and dread had grabbed his breath. He hoped she liked his gift. She hadn't mentioned it when he'd stopped her on the side of the road.

The keys tremble under his fingers as he remembers the photograph he took a few weeks ago in her garden. Jane staring out at him from her house, her dark eyes swimming toward him through the flash, lashes brushing against the lens.

After her father died, there was a trembling in her that drew him closer. A fragility in her movements that made him want to hide her somewhere safe, away from the people that could break her.

He hasn't felt this way since his mother died. This desire to reach through the aperture and touch what he's held inside the frame. He wants to walk beside Jane, to hold her hand as they cross streets and bridges, two of her skips to his one long stride. To hear her laugh, to say her name. *Jane.*

Jane reminds him of a doll. Along with the piano, his mother left him her dolls when she died. After Evelyn's drowning, she scoured garage sales and charity shops to add to her growing collection.

Two years following his mother's death, his father was killed in a car crash and Ernest inherited the house, putting things back where they belonged. Now the dolls sit around the perimeter of his mother's bedroom the way they did when she was alive, leaning against the brocade wallpaper, their legs pressed together primly on the carpet. Evelyn's one-eyed stuffed cat sits on one of their laps. He stands in the middle of his mother's room and turns slowly in a circle, surrounded by dozens of unseeing eyes.

As a child he hated his mother's dolls, but he's grown fond of them since, especially the broken ones. The chipped brunette missing an arm he dropped "accidentally" down the staircase at age three, thumb-sucking gleefully as the ceramic limbs tumbled and flailed. The bald Victorian doll whose golden ringlets perished during his brief infatuation with hairdressing at five. The rag doll he lit on fire at eleven, shortly after his sister's drowning, the cotton skin sooty and singed. Beside the ashen feet lay nine porcelain fingers dangling from a broken wrist. Wiping his forehead between songs, Ernest has the distinct impression he was responsible for this mutilation too.

He stops playing and the unfinished melody reverberates. His mind turns, as it often does, to his mother.

He remembers following her one afternoon as she floated into the bathroom. After his sister died, fear nibbled at the crooks of his elbows, at the back of his neck. When his mother turned, stopping in front of the mirror, he plopped himself beside her bare feet, sunlight streaming in from the window. Her toes were too bony, too blue-white for him to bear. He covered them with his palms, before she gave a gentle kick. "Evelyn," she admonished, absently.

Ernest didn't correct her. He didn't mind when she called him Evelyn. He liked it, in fact. It was a way to keep something of his sister alive. But he wondered what it meant. If, during those moments when his mother called him Evelyn, he was the one who had died.

His mother had stared at herself in the mirror before shedding the high-necked black dress, tights and shawl she wore day after day in mourning. Ernest gazed at her from under the dress that had fallen in a heap on his head. As she stood, impossibly pale in her petticoat, she was the most beautiful ghost he'd ever seen.

After a while, she began pulling brushes, powders, creams and paints out of her drawer. She coloured in her mouth with red lipstick and applied mascara in sweeping, upward strokes, rolling her eyes up until the whites shone.

Each morning that followed, Ernest rushed to the bathroom mirror as his mother's apparition came alive, her cheeks growing pinker, her eyes shining brighter with each brushstroke, each wave of the wand. He knew deep down she was just as cold, just as dead underneath, her leg shivering against his cheek. She'd always worn makeup, but never this much, and never to such transformative effect.

He missed his old mother, the one who played games with them even if she couldn't help but cheat, moving his checkers when he went to the washroom, peeking under the glass table at his cards as she stretched and yawned. He was grateful for her attention and hid that he'd caught on.

He missed his sister too, even though she had broken his favourite toy truck on purpose when no one was looking, whispering, "If you tell…" while furrowing her eyebrows. Another time she had ground her heel into his foot until he screamed, knowing he was incapable of betraying her. She blinked innocently when he was punished but he loved her anyway. The house was better when she was in it.

At fourteen, bored and curious, he'd unwrapped his dead sister's presents, untouched since they were bought for her birthday, three years before. Underneath the paper were two dolls, nearly identical—one with blonde hair and one with black hair mounted on slabs of cardboard. He used his mother's sewing scissors to release them from their threaded handcuffs and played with them guiltily, searching under their dresses for answers.

Footsteps approached. The severed threads were too short to retie. He laid the dolls on the cardboard and snatched the crumpled wrapping paper. The door swung open as he pressed the pink paper down. His mother retrieved the dolls and pressed them to her chest. His father shouted and grabbed him by the neck, shaking him like a cat.

Jane

Annie taps on my bedroom window the next morning with an armful of books, waking me. She probably just feels bad about cheating at Ouija. I crank the window to tell her I'm busy and she can't come over today. She pulls up her hood even though the rain has turned to drizzle. I don't tell her I'm going out or where I'm going. I don't want her to follow me, to ask questions I don't know the answers to.

Her face grows smaller. "Okay," she says, backing into the mist, her face smudged with hurt.

I squeeze into some black flares and line my lids in kohl. I pull on the *Little Earthquakes* concert tee Mom bought me at the Tori Amos concert in Toronto. She's crouching barefoot in a small wooden box, a blue dollhouse piano at her feet.

Annie and I had slipped away from my parents to get a better view and to pretend we were there on our own. Annie liked Tori's wild red hair and the way she didn't care if journalists called her cuckoo for believing in fairies. I was mesmerized by the way Tori straddled the piano bench as she sang, pounding the keys and rocking in ecstasy. It's the shirt I'm wearing in the photo propped on Dad's dresser.

I sulk into Mom's bedroom, craving her arms around me and the sweet citrus of her skin. The bed gapes open. I go to the kitchen, my feet slapping the linoleum but she's not there either.

She won't be back soon, probably not until dinnertime. She's barely around anymore. And when she is, her mind is elsewhere. She even called Groucho "Esmeralda" the other day.

At least Ernest pays attention. His devotion scares and pleases me. There might be something wrong with him. There might be something wrong with me.

I tread through yards, farmland and forest. I shiver when I reach the closest thing Burr has to Bluebeard's castle, edged in wind-battered white pines.

Ernest's front yard is a heap of bobbing weeds and gnarled crabapple trees. I can barely see his once-grand Victorian, just a couple of turrets poking through the fog. I scratch my knees on lamb's quarters and lady's thumb, stepping through creeping bellflower, cocklebur, Queen Anne's lace. My father taught me their names, showed me how to pull them out by the roots from our garden so they wouldn't choke the flowers he planted.

Mud splatters my socks and clings to my soles, making each footstep heavier to lift than the last.

Annie and I came here once before. Some boys in our class dared us to. They watched from the other side of the road, binoculars resting on pimpled noses. We took swigs of Annie's granny's cordial for bravery and pretended we felt something, staggering and raising our voices.

The yard wasn't so overgrown then. We hid the bottle and darted to the ramshackle house easily, flattening our bodies against the wall. The red mansion rose sharply into the sky, a long staircase of cracked stone steps leading up to a small mean mouth of a door. The weathered brick felt cold and rough on our palms and chests and the windows had that rippling kind of glass that makes everything dreamy on the other side. We peeked into each window on the main floor but only saw signs of him having been there—a saucepan rimmed with a crust of baked beans, a doll tossed under a piano, a crumpled suit on the floor. We pressed our ears against the windows, listening.

When Annie ran back to the boys, shaking her head, I felt eyes settle on me like a flock of tiny birds. When I turned he was sitting under a crabapple tree watching me search for him, the shadow of a smile on his face.

What will I find inside Ernest's home this time? I pass under a bower of twisted branches studded with crimson berries that the birds won't eat. As I squint at the windows, I imagine floral wallpaper, racoons peering through the rafters, hidden doors and secret passageways. Bluebeard and a tarnished skeleton key, just for me.

I climb the steps and lift my fist to knock.

Ernest

Ernest opens the door in a pair of striped pyjamas. He's imagined inviting Jane over dozens of times, but always lost the nerve, convinced himself she wouldn't come. She'd said no to him when he'd offered her a car ride and so he'd figured she needed more time. But somehow, even without an invitation, she came.

He grew used to wearing pyjamas at the hospital and now he wears them almost every day. He likes to be ready for sleep to take him down, for his mother's fingers in his hair, for the silhouette of his sister tiptoeing along the skin of his eyelids. But he never imagined wearing his pyjamas while entertaining Jane. He'd pictured himself greeting her at the door in his best black suit at the appointed time, hair parted neatly on the side, a clutch of wildflowers in his hands.

He'd imagined cleaning the house for her: sweeping the floors, attic walls and spiral staircases, pulling out cobwebs, blowing dust off candlesticks and china figurines, wiping the dolls' faces with a corner of the handkerchief his mother had embossed with his initials decades ago.

He wonders if Jane cares that he's wearing pyjamas, wonders if he'll be able to keep his voice from disappearing now that she's right here before him, standing at his door.

A few strands of hair float off her shoulders with static electricity. Her pants look too short, as if she were Alice in Wonderland, shot up on Drink Me.

"Can I come in?"

He gives a slight bow, then ushers her inside. "I apologize for my attire. I was about to change."

She takes off her shoes and follows him through a lantern-lit corridor hung with oil portraits of Ernest's ancestors. Jane and Ernest's shadows bob over the modest bosoms and stern moustaches of the long line of Leopolds, some decades dead.

He leads her to the chintz sofa in the living room, thorns and roses peeking out from beneath the grime. Jane seats herself on the sunken couch.

He hovers over her for a moment. Jane shakes her head as he offers her tea, rye whisky, Orange Crush and a can of sardines, before he remembers his pyjamas, his sleep-tufted hair. He bows again before striding up the spiral staircase in his tattered bed slippers, leaving a faint trail of fluff in his wake.

He dresses quickly but can't find his comb. He dips his fingers under the faucet and runs them through his hair, using a ragged fingernail to carve out a part. He places a Bessie Smith record on the phonograph, moving the needle to the last song, "Graveyard Dream Blues." The vinyl crackles and hisses as he begins his descent, tapping his way down with a cane. Jane turns to watch him spiral toward her in his only tuxedo. As his leather shoes reach the last stair, Bessie opens her mouth.

Blues on my mind. Blues all around my head.

Delight lifts inside him as the music swells. Jane's smiling. She really is. At him.

I dreamed last night that the man that I love was dead.

He leans his cane against the sofa then tugs her fingers until he's pulled her to standing.

I went to the graveyard, fell down on my knee.

He slips his fingers gingerly around her waist.

And I asked the gravedigger to give me back my real good man,
please.

Jane freezes as he starts to move. He stops, lets go.

The gravedigger looked me in the eye.

After a moment, she takes his hands and places them back where they were. She rests her palms on his waist and they sway together, shyly, in a dance.

Said, "I'm sorry lady, but your man has said his last goodbye."

Ernest twirls her and lets go. She spins for a few seconds on her own, in the corner.

He pulls her to him.

I wrung my hand and I wanted to scream.

He stoops so his face is level with hers, their feet moving in tandem under his mother's chandelier.

Jane flushes as he dips her to the carpet, then lifts her up.

But when I woke up, I found it was only a dream.

She releases herself and steps backward. They stand apart with their arms folded, the room crackling.

Meredith

Someone is wearing Henry's eyes. Meredith sweats in her sheets at home, lids flickering.

She walks down the street. Jane, Annie, Ruth, the butcher and the head librarian are standing on the porch of her house, as if assembled for a group picture. When she gets closer she notices their eyes are shut. The wind flaps their hair. As she passes each person, she can feel Henry's spirit unfurling, his blue irises popping open in their faces like terrifying flowers.

She wakes up panting, right hand feeling along her rib cage as if it could soothe the angry beating there. She yearns for her secret forest bedroom. She's been bringing things there each time she visits, steadfastly personalizing the space.

The nightmare happens when she's awake too. The boy in the gas station lifts the flap on her car, filling the tank. When he leans into the window to take her credit card, she looks down at her lap, afraid of what she might find between those fringed lashes.

Only the corneas are transplanted, Meredith had learned at the hospital. Not the whole eyes. But it didn't matter to her dreaming head.

Henry hadn't wanted to give his organs away. He'd had friends who went to med school who'd played with cadavers when the professor wasn't around, flicked bits of brain and bone across the room, high on formaldehyde and their proximity to death. He hadn't wanted to be tossed about, cut into pieces, distributed. He'd wanted to be buried intact.

But he was kind and generous too, Meredith remembered. And when they had taken her into a small room at the hospital and told her good could come out of it, that someone's life could drastically improve, she thought he might have changed his mind if he were there listening to the woman with the clipboard too.

"Maybe," she said.

The woman waited, hugging the clipboard to her chest.

Ernest

The second time Jane comes over, Ernest is expecting her. He's been waiting for her all week. He leads her to his record collection. She sits cross-legged on the floor and pulls out various spines, sneezing at the dust.

"Choose whichever one you'd like," Ernest says.

She settles on an Ida Cox LP. Ernest lights some candelabras. He shows her how to place the record in the player and gently drop the needle. Like the time before, the graveyard blues casts a hypnotic spell, puts them into a trance.

She's more relaxed today, humming along under her breath. He invites her to dance.

"Shall we?" he asks quietly, after the record ends and they've let go of each other.

Jane looks at him.

"Would you like to go to the carnival with me?"

"Right now?"

"Right now."

A heartbeat. And then another. "Okay."

She takes his trilby off the hatstand and places it on her head, bowing to him. Ernest opens the door and Jane steps out under the overcast sky. He follows, closing the door behind him, the record needle still circling its groove.

They strap themselves into Ernest's 1957 Thunderbird as the motor warms up, spewing clouds. As Ernest leans back against the old leather, he gazes at Jane. After a short spell, the engine sputters. They head for London's fairground, muffler clanking behind them down the road.

Jane

I glance at Ernest, mesmerized by his old-fashioned manners and ancient face, the hair on my arms standing on end. As we approach the Western Fair from the parking lot, the sun drops. The screams of children crashing cars and spinning in teacups waft over the cement.

At the ticket window, Ernest unrolls two twenties from his pocket and offers them to the teenager blowing her gum. The pink bubble snaps and retreats as she pushes the tickets toward us. Behind her, rollercoasters race up tracks to the sky.

We stand together inside the entrance, the breeze puffing up our clothes. We could float away if we wanted to, do almost anything. Slow dance suspended in mid-air. Or juggle constellations. Shoot lightning bolts from our palms.

A man stares. I hold his gaze until he looks away, his hand disappearing down the small of his girlfriend's back.

A pair of older teens with matching sun tattoos squirt water guns at plastic clowns, tucking tigers and bears under their armpits when they win. The girl, strong and auburn-haired, looks like an older version of Annie. Ever since the Ouija board fight, we've been avoiding each other at school. I miss her but I'm still mad at her too.

Ernest squints. "It's changed," he murmurs. The game booths' flickering bulbs pulse red, yellow and green on his pale face.

A group of girls my age wearing choker necklaces and flared

jeans turn their heads as they pass, taking in Ernest's old-fashioned clothes. What would they think if they knew we aren't related?

"When were you here last?" I ask Ernest, deciding not to care.

He scans the crowd as if he's lost.

"I've come since I was little," I tell him, raising my voice over the C+C Music Factory dance track. "My dad used to take me and my friend."

Dad's face floats before me when I close my eyes. He waves from a crowd of strangers and I wave back until the rollercoaster takes off, Annie screaming in my ear. I open my eyes. The fairground wavers.

Ernest is watching me closely.

"I came to the fair as a child too," he says. "With my mother and sister. Many years ago."

"Your sister that died."

He turns away from me. After a few moments he points at something in the distance.

"Cotton candy," he says in a small voice.

I lead him through the sunburnt throng, not letting go until we reach the stand.

I dig in my pocket for change but Ernest doesn't let me pay.

"What was it like?" I ask, pulling off a small pink cloud.

"Back then? Everyone wore hats. And the whole place smelled of fried onions.

"There was a lady who sold lavender sachets," Ernest adds, inspecting some neon glow sticks on a table where people are hawking their wares. "And a whole section of handmade quilts."

"There was also a sculpture of the Queen and Prince Philip, carved out of butter." A smile nudges at Ernest's lips. "And a hen in a cage with a sign that said you could play tic-tac-toe with her for twenty-five cents."

He leads me into the agricultural building. "The chicken won."

We catch a sheep-shearing and cow-milking demonstration. I think of how my classmates would laugh. They like to joke that city folk think their milk comes from bottles. They prefer the rural Ilderton Fair to this one. They know almost everybody there and can show their animals and enter the vegetable competitions.

We exit the building and Ernest buys some ride tickets. He asks which one is my favourite. I point to the Gravitron.

"Annie won't go with me anymore," I tell him as we stare at the neon spaceship. "She calls it the Vomitron."

"I'm not quite as spry as I used to be, I'm afraid." He hands me a spool of tickets. "Go. I'll wait for you."

Alone among strangers, I spin inside as the floor drops, the centrifugal force pinning me to the coffin-shaped padded wall, feeling sick and happy, unable to move my limbs, unable to do anything until it's over.

When I stagger out, Ernest says there's a haunted house just around the corner.

I shake my head. "It's just some jerky robots in cages. Not scary."

I point to the Mardi Gras mansion. Annie and I usually skip it because it's mostly murals of jazz musicians and middle-aged people having the time of their life, but I think Ernest might like it.

I take off through the beaded curtains, daring Ernest to catch me. We race down the short metal hallways, pausing in front of funhouse mirrors, dodging children. Ernest almost traps me against a mural of a lady wearing a feather boa and a carnival mask, but I manage to escape. We catch our breath outside in the neon dark, staring up at the Zipper with its screaming teeth.

"Some things are better done away with," Ernest says.

"No one's died on the Zipper in ages," I protest.

He takes my hand and leads me toward the Ferris wheel. "I've been here many times," Ernest admits.

We stand in line, placing the remaining tufts of cotton candy on our outstretched tongues, dissolving them into fizzing lumps of sugar.

"I didn't like the freak show as much as everyone else. Although there was a bearded lady wrestler," he says sadly. "She seemed to be having fun."

"A freak show? Did they actually call it that?"

"There was a fat lady." He pauses, remembering. "And the ossified man who was turning into stone."

"Your turn, sir," says the teenage operator when we get to the front of the queue.

"Thank you," says Ernest, bowing.

We swing our feet as the wheel turns, lifting us off the ground. I hold Ernest's hat in my lap. He whistles, peering down. The tune is familiar: jaunty and a little sad. I can tell when Ernest is impersonating a trombone.

"What are you whistling?"

"'Thinking Blues,' by Bessie Smith. I was playing her record at my house. The first time we danced."

"I listen to old stuff too, but not that old. Mostly '70s, '80s stuff. Bowie. The Smiths. Siouxsie and the Banshees. Do you know them?"

"No," he says.

We don't say anything for the rest of the ride. I'm waiting to wake up from this daydream, or at least waiting for Mom to wake from hers and stop me.

My heart thumps when I think of the unopened doors and secret chambers of Ernest's mansion. As the Ferris wheel brings us back to the bottom, Ernest's cold fingers drum on my head.

"I should take you home," he says, after we step out of the gondola. "You're shivering."

He takes off his jacket and holds it for me to slip into. It's comforting to be in Ernest's jacket, huddled in the folds like a child.

Coattails flap against my bare legs. "I want to keep coming over."

He tilts his head, considering. "We could play hide-and-seek."

I hold his gaze. "I'm good at that."

"But I can disappear," Ernest says. "If I want to."

Ernest presses his hands over my eyes after he parks the car behind the apple tree. I'm not sure if he's being playful or scary. His fingers smell like nickels and cotton candy.

"Come over tomorrow," he says, his voice reverberating in the dark. "Promise?"

My parents used to cover my eyes before revealing a surprise, but if Mom tried that now, I would push her away.

"Promise."

He lets go. I blink at the black dots and smeared light he's made with his palms.

"Goodbye," he says.

At the front door I wave as his car chugs off into the night.

Burr

Burr was once a stop on the Underground Railroad. The locals had helped escaping enslaved persons continue their passage. Had protected them as they journeyed to find freedom elsewhere.

The town's British and Dutch settler makeup hadn't changed that much. But the people believed they could accept difference. They bought wooden furniture from the Mennonites in their bonnets. They tolerated Tiffany Spooner, the U2-obsessed Jehovah's Witness teen who slouched in the hall in her Bono T-shirt for "O Canada," and her unpatriotic family. Paula Valentine, the homegrown girl who ran away from her family and faith only to come back almost two decades later a disenchanted hippie raising two kids out of wedlock. The smart-aleck Western professors with their chickens, Sam and Ella. Ruth's neighbour Jerry Hatt, the socialist with the untended lawn. He didn't dare put up a raised-fist sign.

Ernest

Ernest makes his way from the Thunderbird to his home, humming "Graveyard Dream Blues."

He shambles up the steps and clutches his cane in surprise. Six green glowing eyes.

"Cats," whispers Ernest. He's never seen these cats before, hasn't seen cats around the mansion in years.

The cats are black with white paws and chests and for a second Ernest thinks they are wearing tuxedos too.

"Hello," says Ernest, bending. He trails his fingers along their fur and they press their spines into his hands.

He rustles in his pocket for the key, losing sight of where the darkness ends and the cats' fur begins. The one in the middle has a smudge of white above her mouth.

"Come in?"

They scratch at the door as he turns the key in the lock. He holds it open and they saunter past the oil portraits and into the living room with confidence, as if they've always lived with him.

Where did they come from? Maybe Jane sent them to him, purring directions in their ears. He imagines her performing magic tricks, pulling the cats out of a top hat, one after another.

Or maybe it was Evelyn, incanting spells from above. Dispatching animals to watch over him.

Ernest bends to light a lamp. When he straightens, the three cats are gone.

"Where are you?" His voice echoes.

He waits but the only movement he detects is the grandfather clock's pendulum. After a moment he heads to the kitchen for milk and meat. As he passes the sofa, a paw darts out from underneath, claws shearing his left sock.

"Now, now," Ernest says tenderly to the twinned glints of green, the retreating paw.

He's due for one of his big shops at the discount grocery store in London. He can't find any milk, not even the powdered kind. He sets out three matching bowls of water instead. He opens a can of sardines and the cats come running from their hiding places. After opening two more, he sets all three on the ground. The cats' teeth seize and devour the flesh.

He remembers the patchy feline from his homeless days. Why did she leave him? Why didn't she come back?

Three rough tongues lick the cans clean. He opens more cans. He wonders how the cats found out about him. He wonders how long they'll stay.

Ernest and Evelyn used to sneak strays into the house and hide them from their father. If Father spotted cat ears poking up from the laundry basket or the tip of a tail twitching from under the bedskirt, he'd grab the cat by the scruff and toss him into a pillowcase. He'd pull on his tall rubber boots and go for a walk with the captured feline, swinging the writhing pillowcase as he strode.

Ernest's mother held him and Evelyn back so they couldn't follow. She squeezed her palms over their mouths so they couldn't scream.

Ernest shivers. He focuses on the tuxedo cats right in front of him. Did they catch a glimpse of Jane? Did they like her too?

He hopes she will come tomorrow. "She promised," he tells the licking cats. He'll blindfold Jane and lead her to them, dip her fingers in their moonstruck fur. As if he were a magician and she the trusting audience member, full of anticipation.

He retreats to the sofa when the cats are finished eating. When he sits down, the white-moustached cat leaps on him from nowhere, kneading his thighs. The claws press and curl for phantom milk.

The other two felines slink into the room, licking their teeth. One pounces on the other and they form a ball of fur that tumbles, flashes fangs.

The purring in his lap grows as Ernest pets and he's pleased by the cat's pleasure. He relaxes into the cushions until the cat bites him and leaps off to join the rolling mass. Ernest stares at the two-pronged mark on his wrist. What did he do wrong?

He spies a pair of feet sticking out from under the piano. When he retrieves the doll, she winks at him with one blue porcelain eye. She rustles her dress before turning inanimate again. He backs away on his hands and knees.

He staggers upstairs to his bedroom. There, on his pillow, lies a small animal, freshly killed. It's a mouse, Ernest realizes, mangled and bloody. Warning or gift?

The cats slink up the staircase to see what he'll do. He picks up the stiff tail and tosses the corpse out the window. The cats leap onto his bed, clawing his pillows until they burst into feathers, swarms of tiny white birds.

Jane

I keep my promise, showing up at Ernest's door the next day.

"Follow me," he says, turning on his heel and heading up the stairs. I figure he's leading me to a closet or somewhere else to count while he hides.

Instead, he leads me to the bathroom. His clawfoot tub is full of water, with half a dozen apples sunk to the bottom.

I stare. Does he want me to take a bath?

"It's an apple-bobbing station," Ernest says. "You were robbed."

"What?"

"They should have had them at the fair."

I dip my fingers in the bathtub and tell myself there's no way these are razor-blade apples.

I lower my face into the cold water. My lashes brush through the water as I open my eyes. The bathtub paint is peeling. If Dad were here, he'd be worried about toxic lead. I take a tiny sip.

In fact, he'd be worried about more than the paint.

I focus on a blurry red orb in the corner and let my breath out in a tight stream. My head pounds. There's no air left. Can you still drown in a bathtub if only your head is in?

I shove the apple against the chipped porcelain with my mouth, sinking my teeth in. I give in to my body and its will to live.

Ernest claps as I lift my dripping face.

"I should go." I take a bite of the fruit. "My mom's probably worrying about me."

"We could make candy apples next time," he says thoughtfully. "Although I always found them too sweet."

I listen for Mom when I creep inside. I tiptoe to my parents' bedroom, pausing at the vacant bed before turning into my father's walk-in closet and flipping on the switch.

Everything's gone. The light bulb flickers as I step inside, illuminating the emptiness between flashes of darkness.

I let go of the handle and the door whistles as it swings shut behind me. The hangers expose their wooden collarbones. The nail that hung our framed family portrait reveals itself, glinting its tiny violence on the wall.

The dresser top is bare, speckled only with lint and dust and the imprints of what sat there.

I open the drawers again, willing the familiar contents to reappear. The heavy wool socks, the moth-nibbled sweaters, the flannel nightshirt. The photographs and the letters, the suits and the ties. I crouch, trembling.

The floor no longer carries the weight of his shoes, the burden of his packed suitcase. My fingers fret against the key in my pocket.

I imagine it was my father who took away his belongings. I picture him opening the casket lid and burrowing his way to our backyard through the soil. He wades up through the roses, pushing himself out of the ground. He lets himself in with the key under the mat and slips up the stairs while I'm asleep, sprinkling worms and dirt with every step. His possessions are gone because he needs them. He took his suitcase on a business trip and soon he'll return home.

A thin layer of dust discloses the shape of his soles and the places where his shoes stood, nosing the wall. But the particles are already lifting off the ground, eroding the evidence.

I back out into my parents' bedroom. Things are missing here too. The picture of Dad is gone from the wall.

Someone's trying to rub him out of my home. Someone took his things and I want them back.

It could be my mother. But why would she do this, without warning? Who else would do it?

I punch the faded patch of wall, knuckles straining against skin and drywall. I punch again and again until my skin tears and I yell out. I leave flecks of blood to glisten in the dent I made in the wall.

Meredith

Meredith passes through a grove of American beech trees on her way home after visiting her forest bed. She traces the hieroglyph eyes in the bark, remembering Jane's forest games with Annie, how they crept into the house like feral queens, trailing leaves and dirty footprints, crowns of brambles and matted hair on their heads. They devoured the peanut butter sandwiches Meredith made them in the kitchen, interrupting each other with tales of Wadjet and Bastet, blinking excitedly through Eyes of Horus black liner.

Meredith shared the girls' interest in ancient Egyptians. She was especially fascinated by the cat worship rituals. When she was a child, she'd wished she could have washed Esmeralda's body with palm wine and water from the Nile, removed the liver, lungs, stomach and intestines through a slit in the side of the body, pulled the smashed brain through the nose with a long hook. Rubbed salt to dry out the body and later, stuffed it with sawdust, leaves and linen.

No other child would have painted the strips of linen with pine resin and beeswax more painstakingly than her. No one else would have remembered to place catnip amulets between the layers, or recited the priestess spell by heart to ward off evil.

Esmeralda, mummified and tree-scented, would be placed inside a series of coffins, each one larger than the previous. The third and largest coffin would go inside a sarcophagus carved out of limestone in Esmeralda's likeness.

If she could, she would mummify Henry, she thinks. But who would mummify Meredith? Not Jane—she'd want Jane in the tomb with them too.

As she approaches her house, Meredith quickens her pace. She needs to talk to her daughter. To try to explain what she's found in the clearing in the woods.

As she walks through the living room, Meredith imagines her family's sarcophagi together in the tomb among cherished possessions. A real domestic scene. Slippers near the hearth. Sunday newspaper. Scrabble tiles waiting on wooden racks.

She calls Jane's name. No response. She presses her ear against the locked bathroom door. Her daughter must be showering; she can hear water running. It's late and Meredith is exhausted. Their conversation will have to wait.

She peels off her dress and collapses into her bed. Would she feel protected even then, she wonders, underneath her sarcophagus and nesting coffins and layers of fine linen? (Would she feel safer than when she was alive with Henry, smugly pretending death was something they could will when they were ready?)

Would she and her family pass safely on to the afterlife? Or would it be another kind of limbo, waiting for aliens or archaeologists to dig them up, or a nuclear war to blow them to pieces?

Jane

Mom tried the door while I was showering so I know she's home. I need to find out what's going on with Dad's closet. I pull on my pyjamas and head to her room.

The bedside lamp pours light on her face as she sleeps. She lies on her side in her underwear, splattered with mud.

Her nostrils flare when she exhales. Her breath smells like Groucho's wet food and her armpits are furry.

I take the leaves out of her hair one by one and place them in a pile by the lamp. I leave the burrs in after a few tugs, removing their teeth from my hands. I don't want to go near Mom with scissors while she sleeps.

When I touch the arch in her foot, she sighs. The ends of her toenails are rimmed in polish. I can tell she hasn't painted them red since Dad's heart stopped, probably hasn't clipped them either. They're the longest toenails I've ever seen.

I bet she lit the room for me, knowing I'd come to her in my pyjamas as soon as I woke up. She tossed off the covers on purpose so I would see her growing wild from every pore. My mother, transformed from a woman into a beast.

Her eyelids twitch. I back away from her, repulsed, the questions I came to ask souring my mouth. When she's awake, her toes wrapped in socks, I'll ask her. When I come home from Ernest's, I'll find out where she's been, where Dad's things are.

As the door clicks closed, she murmurs my father's name.

I run downstairs and pull on Ernest's coat. I take a shortcut through the woods to his mansion, the moon lighting my way. The forest growls, blinks with eyes. I push my way through the trees, ducking under boughs and branches until I burst into a clearing by the lake.

"Jane?" the grass whispers. "Is that you?"

Annie's breasts flash through the blades. I think of the last time I saw her almost naked. Our practice kiss. Does Annie ever think about it? Shattered sun on water. Hearts pounding out of our chests. Ernest watching from the long grass as we swam.

Andrew's head pops out of the inside-out shirt he's pulling on. I hate the frosted tips of his hair, and his face—so mainstream handsome.

"Where are you going?" Annie asks breathlessly, buttoning her top. "Are you okay?"

I shake my hair, eyes wet.

"What's wrong?"

"I have to go."

"Is that Ernest Leopold's coat?"

I twist away.

"Jane!"

I take off. Annie follows, ditching Andrew, but I lose her easily, darting behind trees and bushes. When I reach Ernest's mansion, I'm covered in a slick of sweat. I lean against the door, drop the brass knocker three times and count to ten. I have no one else to run to.

He doesn't come. I pound the door with my fist, raw from when I punched my parents' bedroom wall. Count to twenty. I circle the house, but he's missing from every window frame.

"I can disappear," he'd said. "If I want to."

I look for Ernest under the apple tree, where he once crouched, gazing at me. I spy an open window on the second floor. It might be his bedroom. I form a bullhorn and call his name. The curtains ripple but Ernest doesn't appear.

I climb the steps and lie down in his doorway, my cheek resting on the rough stone. When I've almost given up on him, Ernest opens the door and drags me inside.

I hold the enchanted air in my lungs. His home smells the way I'd imagined a haunted house would, all those times I'd huddled around my flashlight reading scary stories past bedtime, wishing for the millionth time that I was the bat swooping in the window, that I was the one turning into a vampire, or at the very least, making everyone scream and clutch their hair.

Ernest helps me up the staircase and takes off my dirty pyjamas. He pulls a flannel nightshirt over my head, his gaze focused on the floor. He folds a sweater for me to use as a pillow and tucks me in, plucking off some feathers. He curls up on the ground.

I push myself up onto my elbows. "You don't have to sleep like a dog."

He sits tentatively on the edge of his bed. "I don't know," he says.

My eyes dart between Ernest's hunched back and the caving ceiling and the single bulb hanging in a birdcage above the bed. I'm afraid, unsure why I am here, why being here is what I wanted. I don't think I'll ever fall asleep until somehow I do and the sleep is dreamless until it's not.

"Ernest Leopold sleeps with the body of a young dead girl," Annie says matter-of-factly. She's wearing Andrew's baseball jersey and nothing else.

Ernest's bed is a casket built for two. I close the lid so Annie can't see inside. I sniff death on Ernest's skin. Our heartbeats suspend as we hurtle through the floors of Ernest's house, plunging into the ground where my father lies, waiting for me.

I wake up alone. The moon is gone and Ernest's bedroom is plain and almost ordinary in the light.

Ernest

Ernest had been sleeping on a bed of feathers when Jane arrived at his door, his mother's mink coat covering him like a blanket.

The cats had pounced on his chest, waking him. He had felt his body return, was aware once more of the springs beneath his limbs. The cats led him downstairs, not to the empty food bowls, but to the doorway. They scratched and yowled.

When he opened the door, he'd discovered Jane sleeping, an apparition dipped in mud. The cats had raced past her, disappearing into the trees.

He touched her shoulder and she stirred, became a real girl. He tried to lift her and was surprised by the weight. He pulled her gently to his room.

She fell asleep on his bed, mouth pressed against his sweater. She had a bad dream and cried out. He sat on the edge, keeping watch. At six o'clock, he crept out of the bedroom, turning his head over his shoulder to gaze at her sleeping face and tripping over her pyjamas.

He took a bubble bath and pulled the dirty clothes into the foamy water with him. He'll clean them for her. She'd like that. The mud bled out of the fabric in thick brown swirls. Her nightshirt floated on the water, whitening, while her pyjama pants crumpled in a blue heap at the bottom of the tub next to his feet. He hung them outside and shuddered when they filled with air, two ghosts swinging side by side on the line.

She comes downstairs while he's reading the newspaper a couple of hours later. He folds the paper and makes breakfast, fried eggs on a bed of Spam. They sit on either end of the dining table, Jane rolling up the sleeves of his pyjamas to her elbows.

"I couldn't find my own," she says, moving food around her plate. Before he can tell her he washed them, she adds, "Dad's clothes disappeared too."

She pierces the egg and it oozes over the can-shaped meat. "The ones in his room." She circles the plate's rim with a yolk-dipped prong.

"Could they be in the laundry?"

"Why would you wash a dead man's clothes?"

Ernest thinks. "In case he comes back?"

Jane stares.

He thinks of something practical. Something his father asked his mother to do, although she'd refused. "To give them away?" he ventures.

Jane shakes her head. "Mom wouldn't do that."

"Maybe she's wearing them?"

"All of them?" Jane sighs.

Ernest rifles through the newspaper to hand her the comics. "*Calvin and Hobbes*?"

"Entertainment. I need to get out of here. Mom, Annie... they're driving me crazy."

They've only been reading for a few moments when Jane gasps. She tears out a broadsheet, using her fingers to smooth out the creases, and pushes it toward Ernest.

The ad is deliberately yellowed and printed in an old-timey font. He takes a magnifying glass out of his pocket and reads:

Alabaster Douglas Drood Presents

"A Night with the Spirits"

September 27, 1994

8 p.m.

His Magical Powers have shocked Scientists and other Skeptics! Many of the learned have been forced by the most overwhelming evidence to acknowledge ALABASTER DOUGLAS DROOD as a True Medium! Musical Instruments are Played; Hands and Arms of Various Sizes Appear and Disappear in full view, plus many other INEXPLICABLE and ASTONISHING Phenomena!*

Prepare to be AMAZED!

Dial 416-555-5555 and you shall receive the secret séance location.

Donation required upon arrival.

---

*No Glittering Apparatus for Deception Used. To preclude any suspicion of the Medium receiving CLANDESTINE ASSISTANCE, The Great Alabaster Douglas Drood and his assistant shall be confined in a Cabinet.

Ernest furrows his brow. He has the fleeting suspicion that the person who wrote the ad is somehow making fun of him, not that he knows Alabaster or anyone at the newspaper. Do séances still happen? He allows himself to feel cautiously excited, intrigued by the promise of unearthly music and the display of magical powers.

"It's tomorrow," says Ernest. "In Toronto."

"Only a couple of hours away," she says, cheeks flushed.

"Oh," he says, sopping up the last of his eggs with a chunk of grey Spam. He hunches over his plate and chews slowly. "You're going?"

"I want you to come with me."

"You do?"

"Yeah."

They smile at each other from across the table.

"I'm not cut out for big-city driving. But I can get us some train tickets for this afternoon."

He lifts his camera from the ledge to take a picture of her as she heads off for school, gamely lifting her legs over weeds and wildflowers. His finger hovers over the shutter release as she grows smaller. Her hair flares in the sun.

He waits too long to press the lever and she's gone.

Jane

When I sit down at my desk Miss Williamson comes over and rests her hands on my shoulders.

"How are you doing, Jane?" she asks quietly.

"Fine." I thrum my fingers on my desk.

"You haven't been coming to class. It's understandable of course, but... If you'd like to talk..." Her sentences drift off.

"That's okay."

"I lost my father last year..."

I watch her fumble for the right words, refusing to give her the teacher-pupil bonding moment she's desperate for.

I hide under my hair for English and Geography.

"Where's your hat?" Andrew whispers when he passes my desk to sharpen his pencil. "Say hi to your old man for me," he says on the way back.

At recess Annie grabs my arm.

"What happened last night?"

"I don't want to talk about it."

"Ernest isn't right."

"Isn't right, how?"

"In the head, Jane."

"I'm not right in the head."

"What does that mean?"

"What am I to you, anyway, Annie?"

Annie storms off. She should get a normal friend anyway,

one who hangs out with boys her own age. I count the remaining time until lunch, will the minute hand to speed its circles on my wrist. At noon, I'll fake sick and slip away to meet Ernest.

Behind the shed, the boys Annie's mom tells us to stay away from push dipping tobacco under their gums, spitting black liquid onto the ground. A couple of jocks smack a ball against the school's brick wall with welted hands. Most of the girls huddle on the grass a foot away, playing some Pi Beta Phi sorority game one of them learned from an older sister called "Good Angel, Bad Angel," a shaming activity Annie and I used to make fun of. This time Annie joins, probably to piss me off.

"I must confess about one of our sisters," Tracy announces from a mouthful of braces. "I saw Tiffany flirting with Shauna's boyfriend at the mall on Saturday. She tried to kiss him in the cafeteria."

The circle gasps, circumference tightening.

"Tiffany, is this true?" asks Angela, class president and uncontested leader of the Burr Elementary Spy Network.

"I guess so," says Tiffany, adjusting her *Achtung Baby* T-shirt.

"Bad angel, bad angel," the circle chants. "Punish her, punish her."

I press my back against the school wall. Crystal Jones appears in a shiny silver shirt and jeans. I avoid her eyes.

"Hi Jane! Where's Annie?"

Her parents are flat-earthers and she's too perky to make friends. Plus, she has old-woman hands, flaky and wrinkled. "Eczema," she says cheerfully when anyone stares. In third grade she poured rivers of salt on her palms and licked them off with her tongue, grinning while we *ew*'d her. We used to hang out, trading troll dolls and Nancy Drews, before Annie moved here.

When she bounded toward us at recess on Annie's second day, Koosh ball earrings swinging from her ears, I stared at the ground while she prattled on. My cheeks grew hot and I felt angry she was making me act this way. I turned away from her when she asked me what was wrong.

Now she says, "Watch how many back walkovers I can do, Jane. Count them. Now."

She arches backwards until her palms press against the tarmac and her head dangles upside down. Her legs lift into the air and pinwheel gracefully over her torso until she's reached the far end of the schoolyard.

I return her triumphant look with a glare.

I bite my nails and gaze at the wide grey sky, praying for rain to fall on Burr, to fill it like an ocean. The church's spire and the flag are the last to disappear as Ernest paddles me away in a canoe, gliding us over uncharted meridians of blue.

When the bell rings for us to go back inside, I hesitate. I wish I could go home and pack an overnight bag but it's too risky. What if Mom is there, and what if she found out I wasn't last night? Anyway, we'll just be in Toronto for one night.

As I drag my heels to my classroom, I pray Ernest's got the tickets to get us out of here.

Meredith

Meredith woke in the twilight, the forest calling her. She longed to head there for sunrise, to see the horizon singed in orange light. Reluctantly, she opened the kitchen window instead.

She needs to talk to Jane over breakfast. She needs to reconnect with her daughter, to find out where she spends her days when she's skipping school.

The squirrels chattered at Meredith through the screen as she set the table for breakfast and waited for Jane to wake up. She watched them dig in the earth as she drank her coffee, burying food for later. In the far corner of the yard, a woodpecker hammered the bark of a dead tree, drilling a cavity to nest in.

Hours passed. Would Jane ever wake up? Meredith stepped out the front door, looking up at the sun high in the sky and the curling wisps of clouds. Mares' tails, a farmer had told her once. Sign of an impending rain.

She re-entered the house and knocked on Jane's door. She fingered the acorns and pine cones she'd been storing in her pockets as she waited. After a moment, she turned the handle.

"Sleeping Beauty," she teased. Her daughter was not inside.

In the evening, a knock. Meredith rushes to the door, hoping it's Jane armed with explanations. An early-morning bike ride and a new after-school extracurricular activity, perhaps.

Her face falls when she sees the group of housewives. They interrupt each other as they share Burr's latest gossip, holding umbrellas over their heads.

When they tell Meredith her daughter was spotted alone in town during afternoon classes, and later, in London's train station with Ernest Leopold, the sticky guilt she's been keeping out crawls in.

She can't remember the last time they spoke. A few days at least. The pain in Meredith's belly grows sharper.

The women's cheeks are pink with excitement. She has the feeling they are enjoying this. Without a word, she slams the door in their faces.

Jane

The train gathers speed, blurring the station and shrinking the waving people into dots.

"Everybody leaves," says Ernest sadly.

"From Burr?"

"From the world."

"I want to go with you," I burst out.

"To the other side? I'm not as old as you think."

"You're older than my dad."

The woman sitting across the aisle lifts her eyebrows over the top of her violet paperback.

"What do you think happens?" I whisper to him.

"When people die?" Ernest whispers back.

"Yeah."

"My sister visits me. She might be in the caboose now, or sitting right here beside me."

"When I saw Dad at the funeral parlour, I didn't think it was him. People say dead people look like they're sleeping. They don't."

The conductor stops beside our seats and takes our tickets, as if discovering Ernest and me together on the Toronto-bound train was the most natural thing in the world.

I gaze out the window, turning my face away from the watchful woman. When I place my hand on the pane, I imagine it's Dad's breath fogging up around it.

In Oakville, Ernest pulls out the sandwiches he made—whole wheat bread slathered in chocolate sundae sauce. We eat them and play tic-tac-toe until our ticket stubs are covered in my *X*s, his *O*s. He grows younger with each speeding kilometre, worry lines disappearing with every town we leave behind.

Near the outskirts of Toronto, Ernest presents two tangerines, offering me one. When I reach over to take it, he winks and the fruit disappears. He pulls it from behind his ear and tosses it in the air. He stands up and begins to juggle, adding more tangerines until six orbit around an empty space.

I unravel the peel in a single piece. The scent hits me: Mom's perfume wafting up my nose. I wonder when she'll realize I'm gone, what she'll do. Will she forgive me for making her worry? Would she read my tea leaves if I came home now, and sing Joni Mitchell to me before I fall asleep? Or will she not even notice I'm gone, or care?

And what about Annie? I'd been her sidekick in all the escape fantasies we'd ever had.

"Are you okay?" whispers Ernest when he sits back down. "Do you want me to juggle some more?"

"I saw Annie's brother Dylan outside the train station. He might have seen me with you."

"We can hide."

"Where?"

Ernest opens a yellowed map of Toronto and sticks it to a chewed gum wad someone left on the seatback in front of me.

"Stand up," he says.

He pulls a handkerchief out of his pocket and ties it over my eyes. "Turn around in a circle. Keep going. Now... Stop! Reach out until you touch—there. Don't move."

I feel a pencil rub against my finger, marking the spot. Ernest takes off my blindfold. "Ontario Place," he says, holding a magnifying glass over the dot. "That's where we'll go."

"Near the highway," I say, reading the black and red lines, the pale blots of blue. "And the lake."

Meredith

As she backs away from the door, Meredith has a vision of her daughter as a little girl.

There's the small rapt face with dark eyes as Henry reads her a Dr. Seuss story on his lap. The excited fingers turning the pages. And the pale legs, kicking in time with the rhymes.

There she is, a bit older, still nestled in her father's lap. Understanding, now, the words he reads. When Henry nods off while recounting a fairy tale, she turns dragon, incinerating him with her breath until he wakes up.

There are the furrowed blonde eyebrows as the crayon is pushed across the paper. The message slipped onto Meredith's desk, begging her to get off the phone and play with her *now*, please.

There's her fine hair fanned out on the white pillowcase as Meredith brings a glass of fresh water to her daughter's bedside table. She switches off the lamp and closes the door slowly until Jane says, "stop," where she always says stop, letting only a trickle of light in. (The last few years, Jane's been getting her own glass of water and closing the door all the way.)

Meredith is dreaming of the bright crack when the phone rings. It's Ruth, asking if she's okay.

She takes a deep breath, inhaling the earth through the open window, after the rain. Jane probably went to the city for some excitement. She's practically a teenager. Ruth must remember.

They were young once too.

Jane could have told her the plan when she wasn't listening. She's been so preoccupied lately. That Ernest sighting was probably a coincidence.

She'll check in with her daughter's friends. They must know something. If not, she'll go to the police. But she doubts it will be necessary. No sense jumping to conclusions.

Meredith's words are measured and rational. She almost believes them herself.

PART TWO

Wearing quetzal plumes
Through eight underworlds
Death comes shining
A thousand bright colours
And music out of this world
Serenades to bony twirls!

—Siouxsie and the Banshees,
"El Dia De Los Muertos"

Ernest

The line behind Ernest and Jane groans and tsks, shifting its feet. "Just get on," grumbles the streetcar driver as they count change on the steps. The streetcar lurches forward; they stumble to the back, past a man muttering curses and a rosary-rubbing woman swinging her feet. The air smells like piss and pizza, like the birthday party they threw for Ernest at Meadowbrook while he was there. The nurses and patients sang off-key around him, an unlit candle wobbling in a whipped-cream rosette.

Jane spins Ernest's hat on her finger and places it on her head. She points out a shirtless man wearing tiny denim shorts, his torso tattooed with Gothic letters, mermaids swimming up his legs. A woman in a batik dress carries a basket of mangoes. Ernest imagines blending the mangoes into juice he and Jane will slurp through bright looping straws.

When the driver slams on the brakes, a small pile of sand spreads along the floor. Ernest starts. Did it come from sandboxes, dispersed by a troop of children's shoes, or was it sprinkled on purpose, to soak up spilled drinks?

Maybe it was Evelyn's doing, the beach coughing up from her lungs. He worries that she'll press her blue face against the windows, the glass doors. Not now. Not with Jane.

The woman counts her beads. The sand drifts.

"Weird," says Jane, staring at the sand, and Ernest realizes she can see it too. It must be real. Unless she's a vision as well. What if he's truly lost it and Jane isn't here at all, doesn't even exist?

"Ernest, you okay?"

He wipes the sweat off his forehead with the back of his hand. "Just hot."

In a magazine left open on an empty seat, a red-lipped brunette pouts in a poster for a movie set during Hollywood's heyday. The image reminds Ernest of being seventeen. Slipping through velvet curtains, his eyes staring into the hot-buttered dark. Ernest isn't sure how he'd managed to sneak into the theatre, but Lauren Bacall on the big screen had been worth it, whatever the cost. Chin to chest, gruffly glamorous, giving Bogey and him "the look."

At the next stop, they get off. Ernest scans the blank-faced mannequins in feather dresses in the shop window on the corner and the photocopied posters of missing cats, trying to figure out which direction to go.

A bearded man pushes a shopping cart brimming with empty bottles and broken toys. Ernest wants to ask if he threw toys down the stairs when he was little, if he takes them out for strolls now to make up for it.

He swallows. "Do you know where Ontario Place is?" he asks instead.

The man points to the hulking overpass. "That way, dude," he says, stuffing a plastic head deeper into the cart with his other hand. Ernest threads his arm through Jane's and hurries them away.

The sparkling spherical dome will be their home base. They'll find some green space nearby to rest for the night. He's heard of communities living under highways. He'll sleep with his eyes open, watching over Jane after the sun sets.

Below the overpass, grizzled grannies cuss. A one-legged man scats for change. Ernest places some coins in his basket. No one looks at them, not even the musician. Ernest wonders if he's disappearing. He pinches Jane's wrist and she pinches his back, but he's still jumpy.

"Let's stop here," he says in front of a red and yellow plastic sign that reads SWELL TIMES.

Dusty lamps bathe the bar in an emerald glow and the jukebox plays Johnny Cash. The bartender hums the melody, her dentures bobbing in a lowball glass next to the till.

"One whisky on the rocks, please," says Ernest.

Jane whispers in his ear. "Make that two," he corrects himself.

The bartender shoots Jane a sideways glance.

A man naps face down at the bar, empty Labatt 50s circling his head like a crown. "This reminds me of a dream," murmurs Jane, as they slide into stools a few spots down. "Only we were with Annie and Siouxsie Sioux in New York City."

"The banshee lady," says Ernest, sliding one glass to Jane and downing his drink in a single gulp.

"You were wearing a leather jacket, like Johnny Ramone." Jane takes a swig and tries not to grimace. "The bartender told us his favourite colour was animal print and gave us a round of shining green shots that tasted way better than Annie's granny's cordial."

Ernest scans the bar. "Is it safe here?" he asks in a low voice. Except for the sleeping man, the bar is empty.

Jane shrugs.

Ernest does what he always does when he feels uneasy. He thinks about music. He decides to tell Jane about his favourite singer, in case she's feeling uneasy too.

"Bessie lost her father when she was young, like you. Her mother too. She fell in love a lot, with men and women."

"She did?"

"People knew," Ernest says. "But she was the Empress. She did as she pleased."

"Did you ever see her?"

"She died a long time ago, in a car crash in Clarksdale, Mississippi." He finishes his drink and orders another. *Slow down,* he tells himself. "Near the crossroads where Robert Johnson sold his soul to the devil."

"What for?"

"Well," says Ernest, considering. "The blues. The devil tuned Johnson's guitar and strummed a few songs before he gave it back. Robert Johnson became one of the greatest blues guitarists and singers that ever lived."

Jane closes her eyes. "I recognize this song."

"That's the Man in Black singing," Ernest says.

"Dad used to play him in the car. I'd complain, but secretly I was into him too."

"Must be strange," Ernest says, "living in your home without him."

She opens her eyes and they gaze at each other in the green light.

"For a while, I thought he was still there, in another room. Or he was on a trip and coming back any moment. I'd listen for his footsteps. I think Mom was listening for them too."

"I know what you mean," Ernest says, telling her how he used to search the closets in the house after Evelyn died, as if they were in the midst of a never-ending game of hide-and-seek.

"What's it like living by yourself in that place?"

Ernest searches his mind. He sees the china dolls and cobwebbed corridors but it's too much like an ordinary haunted house to mention. He hears the jingle of his mother's heavy gold charm bracelet against the banister as if she were alive, descending the staircase in her horse-bit loafers. Inhales the tang of the lemon-squeezed avocados she scooped from the nubbled skin with a spoon. Feels the ivory and sugar-pine piano keys under his fingers, the cat tails curling around his legs as he opens tins of sardines, the half-feral paws kneading his chest as he drifts off to sleep.

"Like home, I guess," he says. "Familiar. And I'm never alone."

"You're not?"

"I have visitors."

"The cats?"

"Ghosts too."

"I want to see Dad's ghost."

"You haven't?"

"Not really." Jane rubs the glass with a fingertip until the condensation disappears. "A couple of dreams here and there."

"He'll come. At the séance, perhaps."

She takes a sip. "I feel alone," she says, "when I'm with other people."

"Ah," Ernest says. "The worst kind of lonesome."

"I don't feel it now though."

Bottles hiss as their caps are wrenched off and Johnny Cash sings "Ring of Fire" over blasts of mariachi horns. The bartender reaches into her lowball and pops in her teeth. "Doing okay?"

Ernest says yes. Maybe it's the whisky, but the bartender is kind of lovely with her dentures in. She reminds him of an older lady he used to know when he was twenty-three. Salt-and-pepper hair falling down her back in loose waves. On each of her arms a row of neat scars, like notches on a bed frame. As if she were trying to keep track of something.

At Meadowbrook, everyone called her Grey. He'd only been there a week or two when she approached him in the patients' garden. She opened her fist to show him a caterpillar with bright yellow bands.

Her children had been taken from her years ago, he remembered overhearing someone say. They used to come for chaperoned visits but she refused to see them. The caterpillar waved its antennae before she closed her fist.

She had more things he might like. Her sea-glass eyes glittered green.

She pulled him through the doorway, the caterpillar tickling Ernest's fingers. There was Fatty, the slug streaking along the common room window, a glowing smear of brie. And Pinky, the baby rat that lived in a shoebox held together with a rubber band. The rodent twitched her nose when Grey removed the lid.

Ernest awoke in the early morning hours to find Grey standing next to his cot. How did she get in? The doors were locked at night. She put her finger to her lips and motioned for him to follow.

She closed the door of her room behind them and lit a candle. Ernest was shocked by her casual use of contraband.

"Undress," she ordered.

He did as she asked, equal parts excited and afraid.

"Now lie down." She pointed to her unmade bed and he obeyed.

She lifted her white nightgown and climbed on top of him. She tipped her head back as she rocked, the tips of her hair brushing his legs. Her breathing quickened and her cheeks shone seashell pink. Ernest hoped he was doing it right. He lost all sense of time in the waves of shame and pleasure.

When she was finished, she dismounted and smoothed the skirt of her nightgown.

Ernest leaned on an elbow. The sheets smelled of salt and sea. He tried not to think of his drowned sister and her missing body washing up on the rocks.

"What's your real name?"

She stared at him as if that was a stupid question.

He touched her beautiful hair.

"Don't get attached," she said, removing each finger.

The next morning Grey wasn't in the garden, cafeteria or common room. Fatty and Pinky were gone too. The door to her room was locked. No one answered his knocks. He returned a couple of hours later and the door was open. The room was being vacuumed. The mattress wrapped in a teal plastic cover.

"How old do you think I am?" Ernest asks.

"One hundred and two?"

"Sorry to disappoint you, but—"

"Shh, don't tell me. I want to believe I'm friends with the oldest man on earth."

The blacked-out man raises his head. He lifts each empty bottle as if someone played a trick, as if it wasn't him who drank them all. "Hey," he says.

Jane half turns her face.

"What's going on?" the man asks her.

"Just talking to my friend."

"This 'friend' bothering you?"

"No," Jane says.

"I'm sorry if I woke you," Ernest says, letting go of Jane's hand under the bar.

"You're a bit old for her, aren't you?"

"I want to go," Jane whispers to Ernest.

"I'm just having a conversation with you." The man laughs.

The bartender wags a finger. "Leave them alone, Jimmy."

"I'm afraid I can't do that," he responds.

"Why not?" Jane says.

Jimmy scoots his stool, stretching his neck until his face is only a few inches from Ernest's. "I. Don't. Like. Creeps," he spits.

Ernest wishes he were a different kind of man. Someone people respected. Someone who could defend himself. A man like his father. No. A man like Bogart. He wants to get off the bar stool but can't, feels a numbness spreading through his body, as though he were turning into ice.

"Back off," Jane says.

Ernest is wondering how to de-escalate the situation when the crunch of Jimmy's knuckles on his jawbone knocks him off the stool. He crumples into a heap at Jane's feet, his head full of pain and pressure.

He opens his eyes. Her face is hanging over him like a supermoon. She pulls him to his feet and slings one of his arms over her shoulders, helping him hobble between the rickety tables and chairs. When unsteady footsteps come up behind them, they hurry out of there.

Water soaks through Ernest's socks and pools in his trouser pockets as they run through the rain. His jaw throbs and his eyes burn. He glances at Jane, at the rain dripping off her nose and chin, at the droplets clinging to the fine down of her skin.

Befriending Jane has given him a second chance. A reason to keep going. He won't muck it up this time.

Meredith

After filing a report with the police department, Meredith trudges home. When she opens the door, the telephone is ringing. She sprints toward it, freezing when the black pixels spell out Ruth's name on the caller ID screen.

Meredith doesn't pick up. She can't handle her friend's questions or concern right now. She covers her ears to block out the voicemail with its panicked pitch.

The message clicks off. She dials Annie's home. Her daughter's friend answers and Meredith asks if she remembers anything. When Annie says no, Meredith thanks her, rushing to return the handpiece to the cradle.

Meredith makes herself a sandwich. She doesn't bother washing her hands or defrosting the bread. She can't be troubled to get a knife from the drawer. She uses her index finger to spread peanut butter on the freezer-burned bun.

She leans against the kitchen counter and chews, barely tasting her dinner. She leaves the crusts on the counter for the ants and wipes her hands on her shirt. Groucho is nowhere to be seen but Meredith fills his food bowl and pours him fresh water anyway. She'll deal with the litter box later, she tells herself.

Meredith doesn't want to go into her daughter's bedroom, but her feet stop outside the door anyway. She watches her fingers reach to turn the knob. The door whines as it swings open. She flicks on the light and dust particles drift through the air.

Meredith walks around the room slowly, trailing her finger-tips across the bookshelves and the Magic Eye poster that never revealed its secret image to her, no matter how she focused her eyes. No signs of Ernest and no clues as to why her daughter would run away with him. A rumour, she reminds herself.

On Jane's desk, below some sticky goblets, lies a three-card tarot spread. Did Jane leave this for her as a clue?

The left card depicts a man carrying ten wands. His back is hunched, head bowed. The wands are heavy, but he is resolute, carrying them toward some sort of village or city.

In the centre, a bright-red heart hovers in a thunderstorm, pierced by three swords.

On the right, a black crayfish waving its claws out of the water, a wolf and a domesticated dog barking at a dejected moon.

The cards seem ominous, but Meredith knows from the limited knowledge she has of tarot that there is more than one way to read them.

Meredith turns off the light and peers at the constellation of glow-in-the-dark stars Jane stuck on the ceiling when she was ten. A sick feeling crawls up her hip bones and into her belly.

She thinks of her pregnancy. How she pored over baby books to learn about the swimming fetus with the shrinking tail. Each week, the baby's size was compared to something edible: a peppercorn, a Brussels sprout, a nectarine.

She'd worried she was gaining too much weight. Then worried she wasn't gaining enough. As she threw up in the toilet, she'd feared her baby was being deprived of essential nutrients.

Don't worry, the OB/GYN had said. In utero, the fetus would be fine, leaching whatever it needed from her bones if necessary.

"Like a parasite," Meredith had blurted out. When he looked horrified, she laughed as if she'd been making a joke.

In the beginning, she'd detested pregnancy. Couldn't stand the ruffled floral sacks she had to wear after she'd outgrown all of Henry's clothes. She disliked the other soon-to-be mothers who spoke to her in a singsong voice as if she were a baby too. It was tiresome. The constant checkups and measurements and questioning. The lists of what she couldn't eat, couldn't drink, couldn't do.

At a party, Henry's colleague reached out and caressed her belly as if it were public property. As if her body was no longer hers.

It wasn't. She felt betrayed by the nipples that grew erect at every urgent high-pitched sound. By the milk that flew out in the direction of any crying baby, leaving two cold wet spots on her shirt.

The bigger Meredith grew, the more Henry desired her, licking her gleaming skin and squeezing her ass. They made love fervently, while inside Meredith's uterus the baby punched and kicked and grew.

Toward the third trimester's end, Jane's fists and feet pressed against the walls of her womb. Meredith wondered if her baby was dreaming of separating from her body, if she was ready to be thrust, slimy and screaming, into the world.

Henry had been in the basement polishing shoes when Meredith's water broke. He ran up the stairs when she'd cried out. Amniotic fluid streamed down her legs as they walked together to the car through the snow.

In the delivery room, she'd fixed her eyes on Henry's, his steady gaze sustaining her through the radiating rings of pain, giving her the courage to push.

When their daughter had emerged wet and hollering from between Meredith's legs, they'd been amazed by the wide-eyed creature they'd created, kissing the soft misshapen head and purplish legs. As Meredith held her baby for the first time, she'd felt as though her heart was beating outside her body. The *linea nigra* took two seasons to fade, a reminder of the way Meredith's body had been irrevocably split into two.

For months after giving birth, Meredith's belly had hung like an empty sack. Milk swelled in her breasts and dripped from her nipples, her body transformed into a dairy operation that burbled along without her conscious participation. Its brisk efficiency confounded her. Her body was a factory, concerned with inputs and outputs, devoted to the mind-numbing, repetitive task of feeding.

She feared that her body had lost its sensuality. She was constantly thirsty. Her lips were chapped and her vulva dry. Jane was a barracuda, her mouth open and hungry, coming for her and stealing all her moisture. As Jane grabbed at the buttons of her shirt and tore at her bra, Meredith could sense the razor teeth hidden in the gums, waiting to break through.

But she feels a tenderness now when she remembers Jane rooting instinctively along her breast. She yearns to hold infant Jane against her body, the warm bum nestled in her palm, wrinkled hands tangled in her hair. She misses her daughter's milky breath. The piglet squeals and angry baas, the panting as Meredith unlatched the cup on her nursing bra. Her head, fuzzy as a newborn chick's. She misses Jane's pure, pink delight as she pulled off the nipple to look at her, milk dribbling down her chin.

Meredith hadn't let her out of sight. She'd carried her everywhere in a stretchy wrap, binding their bodies back together. When she tossed a jacket of Henry's over their combined bodies, their silhouette became reassuringly pregnant again.

Part of her had loved being needed. Her daughter twisting herself toward her, as if she were a plant and Meredith the sun. She was proud to be the only one who could nourish her.

But she hated being needed too. Her breasts were punitive toward her, hardening between feedings. Jane cried unless she was held, so Meredith found herself spending hours on the couch, tea cold and curdled, beloved books out of reach. She resented the boredom and constant demands, the monotonous soundtrack of her slippers padding back and forth down the hallway to change Jane's diaper and rub the stains off her miniature clothes. Poop regularly escaped the diapers Meredith clothed her in, the brown silhouette of Italy surfacing on her leggings.

Meredith was envious when young girls sauntered by her window, off to read under a tree or rendezvous with a lover. During these moments, she felt acutely the weight of her babe in her arms.

In the colicky evening hours, as she stared at the quivering triangle of flesh at the back of her daughter's red throat, Meredith felt certain she would never be able to give enough, that she wasn't capable of quelling her daughter's insatiable needs. In her bleakest moments, she wondered if she were slowly being eaten alive.

"It's normal postpartum," Henry said, stroking her hair.

"Is it?" she asked, rage coiling snakelike inside her.

"You just miss having your baby inside you."

"How the hell do you know?" she'd hissed.

Anger flared easily that first year. She relished the heat and power of it. She was more fully herself in ways she hadn't been before.

Her behaviour frightened her too. This was one reason why conversations about having more children had been fraught. Henry wanted another, and Meredith knew Jane would eventually want a sibling too. Meredith herself had hated being an only child and felt guilty inflicting that particular loneliness on her daughter.

But she couldn't go through the postpartum madness again. The jags of uncontrollable sobbing. The hair falling out. The insomnia. The time she hurled Henry's favourite mug against the wall. (She couldn't remember now what he'd said.) Jane, bawling from her high chair. Meredith had cut her hands picking up the shards.

How could Henry consider another child, now that she'd finally started to get her life back, had begun to muster some self-control once more?

She'd been more than ready when it had come time to switch Jane to solid foods, and thankful when her body had somewhat, but not completely, reverted to its pre-pregnancy shape. She was grateful to have her body return to her.

But had it really?

Standing alone in her daughter's room, she experiences a phantom kick. Meredith grasps the bookshelf to steady herself. Out of the corner of her eye, she sees something slither in the dark. She trembles, wondering if umbilical cords have ghosts.

Jane

The rain thins and stops. The neighbourhood is harsh and ugly, a string of tail lights pulsing red.

"What should we do?" Ernest asks, turning his face toward me.

"Ernest—watch out!" He narrowly avoids a telephone pole and careens into a woman eating Goldfish crackers in an electric wheelchair, almost hitting her in the face with his cane.

"Sorry!" he says, before breaking back into a jog.

The woman toots her horn and swears.

We twist our necks every few steps until we're sure no one's following us from the bar. Gradually, the running starts to feel okay, like I'm stomping out what that scary man said, making the city safe for us. We run down the sidewalk because we want to now, leaping over puddles and rain-drunk earthworms, storefront awnings dripping on our heads.

After Dad's funeral, I thought about being a worm. A tiny tube of grief, stuffing my mouth with soil. I wanted to feel the earth pass through my body as I tunnelled underground. I wouldn't have eyes anymore but it would be too dark in the casket to see Dad anyway. I could wriggle up the sleeve of his suit and lie on his embalmed chest and breathe him in through my new purple skin as he started to decompose and my boneless friends nibbled him. And if life ever cut me up again, I could grow a new head or tail, easy.

Ernest and I slow down, gulping for air. I step carefully over another earthworm.

"If the Christians are wrong and reincarnation is real, then I'll be an invertebrate in my next life and wear my skeleton on the outside," I tell Ernest.

"I'll be a worm with you. That, or a shiny black crow."

The street glistens, giving off a humid energy. Music swells as a ten-person marching band overtakes us, glittering knees lifting in unison. The feathers in their tall caps are dripping and their makeup is smeared from the rain.

A young woman in a black vinyl trench with pink buns all over her head films the action with a Panavision movie camera. She reminds me of Annie, if Annie wasn't so tall and had never left a big city. The woman doesn't care we're in her frame and I wonder if she's a guerrilla filmmaker or a music video director.

I kick-box the air when I realize what the band is playing. "Tori!" I shout to Ernest.

A different rhythm snakes in and "Cornflake Girl" morphs into Björk's "Big Time Sensuality."

"Come on," says Ernest. He enters the parade and I follow him.

"Careful, girl," says the leader in a baritone, huge blonde curls bobbing behind her. She has peacock-feather eyelashes and the most glamorous legs.

The marching band fans open, creating a V-formation. I spy Ernest at the back. I dodge trumpeters and clarinet players to get to him, shouting along to the lyrics as the stars turn on.

Ernest hoists me onto his shoulders and I twirl his wooden cane over my head like a baton.

When the song ends, Ernest tosses the drum back to the marcher behind him and I slide down his back. We split off from the skein and spot an atrium hidden behind a grove of trees. Ernest kneels beside a puddle and I crouch beside him.

We look down at our wavering faces. Ernest reaches into his pocket and pulls out his ticket stub from the train. He folds it into a miniature crane and places it on the water's surface. After a few seconds, he pushes it forward, lets go.

I press my hands against Ernest's curved-in chest, feel the drum roll beating there.

Burr

The way Burr was panicking, an outsider might assume Jane had disappeared weeks ago.

The townspeople plan "Save Jane" meetings in basements and churches. They speak of bake sales. They test the word *abduction*.

They interview Annie and the girl with Evelyn's shoes. They send the tape to London's TV station with a note: *Help Burr find our Jane!*

They warn their children, who doodle along the margins of their notebooks, feeling important as well as scared.

He's a line drawing on Jane's empty desk, his spine curved like a scythe.

He's a shadow stretching over the sidewalk on their way home from school. He's a scarecrow dressed in their parents' rags.

He's a miser. He's why you shouldn't leave your children a large inheritance. He's a millionaire who dumpster dives for dinner.

He's a Boo Radley wannabe. He's a hundred-year-old vampire. He's a garage-band song sung by teenagers desperate to save someone.

On the second day of Jane's disappearance, the police swarm Ernest's mansion. They move from room to room, examining his notebooks with gloved fingers.

They leave messages for Meredith on her machine. They think about her dead husband, the former wrestler. The one hundred push-ups and the claps in between.

Meredith

Meredith pours coffee for the plainclothes officer sitting at her kitchen table. Her hand is shaking, which causes the coffee to run down the outside of his mug and splash on the table.

She's aware of his eyes as she wipes up the mess. If she comes across as guilty, it's because she is.

Ruth said she would take a day off work to be with her for this meeting. Meredith wishes now that she'd relented. Her stupid pride getting the better of her. How could she think she could carry the weight of this on her own?

She's never been in trouble with the law—she's privileged enough to have had limited interactions with the police. Parking violations, mostly. The odd speeding ticket.

What if she doesn't answer the questions correctly? In the best of times, she's a dreamy person, someone who searches for missing sunglasses while they're perched on the top of her head, prone to forgetting birthdays, to completely losing track of time.

The cop takes a sip. Is his sympathetic look a ruse, a ploy to encourage her guard to come down? With that baby face, he can't have been on the force for long.

"Any ideas as to why your daughter might have left town?"

Meredith shudders as he breathes the familiar question into the air. It's been hanging over her since Jane disappeared, but that doesn't mean she has a good answer.

"Anything at all?" he presses, pen hovering over his notebook.

She struggles to answer. Her response, when it comes, is vague. Jane's been grieving for her father. They both have. Such a shock. Not themselves.

A memory overtakes her. Jane's pale face on the other side of the shovel's spray, her father's casket carefully lowered underground.

She'd felt like a new mother after Henry's death, overwhelmed by Jane's sudden, suffocating need. Overwhelmed by the space she craved. She told herself as she retreated that it would just be a temporary break.

In the newspaper column on common grief symptoms that Ruth had Scotch-taped to Meredith's fridge, *Numbness, remoteness, depression* shared a single bullet point. *Dissociation (intense feelings of unreality, denial and detachment)* formed another.

Meredith knew these symptoms intimately. She hadn't really tried to bridge that impossible emotional distance. And now Jane was actually gone.

"Any ideas where she might be?"

"If I knew, then we wouldn't be having this conversation," Meredith says, unable to keep the anger out of her voice.

"Any place that would have special meaning for her?" the officer persists. "Or somewhere she wanted to visit?"

"Well, she had this dream of going to Egypt to see the tombs and pyramids. And more recently, she wanted to move to New York City to start a band. But what teen into punk and rock 'n' roll doesn't?"

"What about Mr. Leopold?" he presses. "Any reason they'd go somewhere together? We believe she may have boarded a train."

Meredith flinches. "They happened to be at the train station at the same time." She pours cream into her cup, watching it swirl and disappear. "But that doesn't necessarily mean anything."

"So you don't think they were leaving together?"

"A lot of people take trains."

"Not recluses."

"Not usually," Meredith concedes, stirring in a spoonful of sugar, about to throw up.

"Annie says there's something going on between them."

"I don't know about that." Refusing to admit her daughter has run away with Ernest doesn't prevent it from being true, but it's a powerful impulse, all the same.

The officer searches her face.

"Those are just rumours," Meredith says, bile rising in her throat.

"Well," says the officer. "You have our card. Please check in every day. And if something comes back to you before tomorrow, no matter how trivial, give us a ring immediately."

"I'm sorry you're going through this," he adds as he puts his arms through the sleeves of his coat. "So soon after the loss of your husband."

Meredith realizes with a start that she knows him. Kyle Van den Bergh. A long time ago, before his family moved to London, he used to come to the library with his mother. His arms were never big enough to take home all the books he wanted and he threw terrible tantrums when it was time to leave.

"Your husband let me come and fish when I was going through a tough time," Kyle says now. "He was a great man. Larger than life."

"Thank you," Meredith says. She'd always thought that was an odd thing to say about someone but maybe it was true.

As she leads him to the door, Meredith realizes she's making weird sounds. For once she's aware of it. She bites her tongue to stop.

She wonders if the officer heard her strange hums during the interview and if so, what he must think. Some kind of throat infection, hopefully. Henry had affectionately called them the Gremlins. Jane, half-jokingly, claimed her mother was possessed.

Meredith usually only had the Gremlins when she was wearing headphones and concentrating. Henry had imitated her at the dinner table one evening, but Jane shook her head and said that wasn't right. She retrieved a secret cassette recording from her bedroom and slipped it into the boom box, dialing the volume of her mother's subconscious soundtrack up to max.

Meredith had laughed with her family, wanting to be a good sport. But deep down, the noises frightened her. It was as if there was an animal trapped inside her, trying to speak out. Could that be the voice of her true self?

She thanks Kyle for searching for her daughter. On the front porch, another casserole, smothered in tin foil and taped with a neighbourly note. She shoves it into the fridge, hoping there won't be more. She's already got a freezer full of charitable meals. It's presumptuous. Jane's alive.

Jane

In Dad's eyes, I was constantly surrounded by danger. He was always dialing down the volume on my Sony Walkman and telling me to get away from the microwave. I'd be nuking some pizza pockets for a snack and he'd come into the kitchen groaning, "No-o-o-o," before grabbing me by the waist and lifting me high, away from the invisible rays.

The microwave didn't frighten me. I liked the way the spotlit food spun around on its glass pedestal, and I enjoyed Dad's sincere rescues too. I lip-synched along to his lectures.

I leaned my chair back against the island in the kitchen so only two legs remained on the floor. I observed him from half-closed eyes as he winced and gestured. I tilted further and he mimed my head splitting open and blood trickling out—each finger a tiny red river.

When I was seven, my parents lost me in the mall. We'd been there for ages and I was bored of them rifling through the racks. In some clothing store that isn't around anymore, I'd pulled on their sleeves and begged to go home, but they'd said, "Patience."

I wandered into an empty dressing room, closed the curtain behind me and sat cross-legged on the floor.

For some reason, there were sewing pins stuck in the carpet and I arranged them into spirals, suns and stars. My fingertips pinged with static electricity. I was putting the finishing touches on a pin portrait of Groucho when a birdlike woman clawed back the curtain.

"Oh!" the woman said, smiling, a pyjama set draped over her arm like a flannel wing. "Playing by yourself, eh? Wish my kid would do that."

She closed the curtain and went into the stall next to mine. I sat on the floor for a long time, but no one else came in.

I grew tired of the pins and the feet that strode past my change room and the oohs and aahs of the saleswoman stationed by the mirror. I stared at the undisturbed curtain and felt angry with my parents for not coming to get me. I left the dressing room and searched the store, my eyes tracking up denim legs and parkas. I couldn't find Mom or Dad anywhere.

I stood in the middle of the store and surveyed my surroundings. A saleswoman with frizzy yellow hair arranged cardigans on a wooden table while her balding co-worker rang up purchases for the customers standing in line. No one noticed me. I walked to the pyramid of sweaters and looked into the saleswoman's powdered face. She continued folding the nubby wool into bricks, as if I wasn't there.

I held my breath, lightheaded, wondering if I'd somehow become invisible. I was a ghost with a silky white body and holes for eyes.

I took a deep breath and flew into the wall. The salespeople rushed over at the sound of my body smacking into bricks and clattering to the ground.

I rubbed my head. The salespeople stared. The man ran to the phone and spoke rapidly into the mouthpiece while the mirror lady fed me water out of a paper cup and held up fingers for me to count. Two, four, three. She aahed encouragingly, like I'd tried on an expensive dress.

My parents ran through the door. Their cheeks were bright pink, as if someone had pinched them.

"Thank God, thank God, thank God," Mom said. She gathered me in her arms and I pressed my face against her parka. Her heart pounded through nylon and feathers.

As soon as we left the store, Dad said, "You can't do that, Jane. You scared the hell out of us."

"Henry," Mom said.

Dad went quiet. A minute later, he reached out to stroke my hair. I nestled deeper into Mom's puffy arms so he could only touch a small part of my head.

"He's just scared," she whispered in my ear, "because he loves you."

"Why didn't you call my name?"

"You were there, and then you were gone. We freaked out."

Mom and Dad took me to the Chinese restaurant in the mall that we usually only went to for birthdays. It has folding lacquer screens with fancy painted ladies on them and tanks of Siamese fighting fish that ripple like swatches of frayed silk.

Mom chose all of my favourite dishes—platters of spring rolls, pork fried rice and chicken chow mein—and Dad ordered me a Shirley Temple. I should have been happy but I wasn't. Everything tasted weird. The food was too greasy and the salt stung my tongue. My parents were watching me in a way they never had before. I wished I were still in that change room, pushing pins into the floor. I couldn't believe Dad had been angry with me when they were the ones who had left me behind. I chewed the maraschino cherry off the plastic sword and spat it out.

Even then, I knew what they were worried about. I knew kidnapping existed. That some men would try to lure you with candies. That the real monsters were human in form.

A couple of years later, I hid in the coat closet as Mom retold the shopping mall disappearance story to Ruth. I'd wanted to be reassured they hadn't left me on purpose. I was curious where they'd gone.

While Mom was talking with security, Dad had exited the mall. When she spotted him near the parking lot, he was peering in the backs of cars. He even lifted the lid of a garbage bin.

Ernest

The sun rises, flooding Ernest's eyes with warm yellow light. A lady wearing a tattered wedding veil tosses bits of bread at the pigeons. She squints at Jane curled asleep beside him on the bench. "Granddaughter?" she asks.

Ernest doesn't want to wake her. He nods and the woman drifts away, birds trailing her ankles.

He's jumpier than usual. Sure, Ernest has seen Evelyn since she died, but the doctors at Meadowbrook told him it wasn't really his sister, instead the result of a temporary psychosis stemming from childhood trauma and a sickness in his brain.

If his dead sister shows up at the séance, it will be different. She can't be a figment of his imagination, Ernest supposes, if other people can see or hear her too.

What will Evelyn be like? Will she talk to him? Will she be translucent? Will she wear white shoes? Do ghosts have feet or do they float off the ground, ankles dissolving into mist?

Will she have aged while dead, an old woman trapped in a little girl ghost? (He has trouble, as always, imagining her this way.) Or will she be how she was on her last living day, trampling his sandcastle, racing in and out of the waves? The way she is when he senses her all around him, taunting him with childish glee?

Will she recognize him after so much time has passed? Will she let him hold her in his lap as he explains why he didn't save her? Will she listen as he begs for forgiveness? Will she even show up?

Ernest is lightheaded from all the possibilities. He grips the armrest and thinks of what the séance might be like for Jane.

He pictures the Great Alabaster Douglas Drood as a younger, cooler Henry, who can beckon any spirit whenever he pleases. In Ernest's mind, he has spiky black hair and a python flung around his neck like a scarf. Jane, fascinated, asking lots of questions post-séance about psychic frequencies and snake care while floating tambourines jingle and shake.

Ernest wonders if the medium is taller than him. Whether he can juggle more oranges. If he can levitate.

He imagines Jane stretching up on her tiptoes to gain a better view of Alabaster's impressive moustache. Then she's levitating too.

A warm tongue washes over Ernest's lips. He raises his gaze to the black nose of a dog. The dog's eyes are dull and his ribs protrude. His owner is nowhere in sight. If he has an owner. Ernest reaches out to pet the dog, but the animal shies away, his tail heavy and matted.

Ernest picks the crusted sleep out of his eyes and tries not to think about what will happen when they run out of money. He tries to forget the mattress stuffed with cash at home. He wishes he'd brought more money, wishes he'd brought all that's left of his inheritance.

He concentrates on the warm weight of Jane's head on his chest and the shelter he's forming for her right now with his body.

City crows memorize the routes of garbage trucks, growing fat from French fries but somehow extending their life expectancies. Songbirds pack their nests with cigarette butts to protect their young, repelling parasites with nicotine. If birds can adapt to modern civilization, why can't he?

Jane

I grip the phone receiver. "I'd like to RSVP for tonight. Two people for 'A Night with the Spirits.'"

"I'm sorry, but it's sold-out," says the man.

My palms sweat. "We've travelled hours to attend. Is there any way—"

"We've scheduled another séance for tomorrow afternoon," he interrupts. "You're in luck." He gives me the time and address. A click and he's gone.

"Are you okay?" asks Ernest.

I put down the phone. "We can go to the séance tomorrow. Which is actually Dad's birthday."

I can't believe it's been a whole year since he turned forty-two. I'd helped Mom with the cake. A relic from the '70s that was my father's favourite, even though it was a Bundt and not the usual birthday-cake shape. A Harvey Wallbanger with glugs of orange juice, Galliano and vodka and a base made of powdered yellow cake and instant pudding mix.

It wasn't a milestone birthday and no one knew it would be his last. We belted out "Happy Birthday." It was nice in a casual way. The kind of day I miss most.

Ernest taps me on the shoulder, asking again where we should go.

"Follow the map?" I suggest. "We never made it to the place I picked when you blindfolded me on the train."

He nods. "Ontario Place."

"I have to make another call first though."

I dial home. Mom's hello reverberates in my ear.

"Jane? Where are you?" I picture her collarbones surging under her skin.

"Are you okay?"

I'm about to tell her when I see her muddy feet hanging off the bed.

Where are you, Mom? Where have you been?

"Jane, where are you?"

Where are you? sway the hangers in Dad's closet.

Where are you? tap Dad's empty dress shoes, moonwalking backwards through the dust.

"Don't look for me," I say and hang up.

Meredith

Meredith stands in the living room with the phone in her hand. She tightens her fingers around the dead line.

Where the hell is my daughter?

She should inform the police right away. But Jane's warning echoes in her ears.

The doorbell rings. She creeps to the door and presses her eye against the peephole. She backs away slowly, so the neighbours on her doorstep won't know she's home.

She slumps onto the carpet and stares at the wall. Minutes pass. The doorbell rings again. The ringing sounds distant, as if it were happening in another woman's house, on behalf of another woman's missing daughter.

She once saw a TV program about an artist who translated *Moonlight Sonata* into Morse code, bounced it off the moon's surface and translated it back into music. In the art installation, a piano played the moon-battered music by itself. Meredith shudders as she remembers the keys moving up and down, hears the pocked silences and imperfect melody—familiar, yet damaged from its brief encounter with outer space.

Will Jane be different when she comes back?

If she comes back, replies a tinny voice in Meredith's head.

She needs to get out of the house.

The neighbours go home. After peeking through the window to make sure they're gone, Meredith exits the house, leaving it unlocked for Jane. She sidesteps the new casseroles on the doorstep and hurries to the forest, urged on by a hope that something will be revealed there.

The police believe Jane left town, but Meredith can't stop thinking of her daughter's forest games with Annie. She can't help listening for her footsteps among the trees.

She trails her fingers through the leaves but hears only the caws of the crows, their beaks scooping seeds and insects, twigs for their nests.

Find her, rustles the forest.

She turns back before she reaches the clearing, breaking into a run.

Ernest

Jane and Ernest enter Good Life Chinese Food Restaurant and sit down. Ernest taps out a Sister Rosetta Tharpe guitar riff on the lemon Formica table, while other old-timers converse in their mother tongues, teacups rattling in arthritic hands. On the TV hanging above them, a man in a trench coat announces a warm front coming in.

Ernest is grateful. There's been a chill in his bones recently that he hasn't been able to shake. Outdoors, indoors, jacket on, jacket off—it doesn't matter.

"Temperatures expected to rise throughout the week," the meteorologist promises before the program cuts to a commercial for Gas-X.

A blonde woman in a cobalt bathing suit sits in a white lounge chair. "I may look like this," she says, pointing to her svelte body, "but I feel like *this*." Her eyes fill with horror as her face and belly swell.

Ernest is transfixed by the lady's new body. It reminds him of Jane in the Mardi Gras funhouse, chasing him past the pulsing bulbs and orange slide, up the staircase with its murals of balloons and clowns and a man playing a trumpet solo, along the wall of mirrors, each one encased in a black and white piano keyboard frame. Ernest catching sight of Jane in pursuit, her image stretching and warping past recognition. Ernest's too. So much has happened. It's hard to believe that was only a couple of days ago.

The white powder solution fizzes and pops. After drinking the potion, the woman's body morphs back to its original size. "I feel like me again," she exclaims.

Jane pours lukewarm tea from the pot. They sip and Ernest waits for the meteorologist to return. He hopes for more good news, for the sun to burst from behind the clouds and warm his skin through the restaurant glass.

But the meteorologist's mood darkened during the commercial break. "Ozone hole suspected cause of surge in sheep blindness and rabbit cataracts," he says now, as a herd of Chilean sheep walk into a fence.

Ernest reaches in his pocket and takes out a pair of heart-shaped plastic sunglasses. "I found these in the park this morning," he says.

"Sometimes I wish humans would get wiped out," Jane says with a dramatic sigh, putting the glasses on as bunnies with opal eyes hop crookedly across the screen. "Sucked into a giant sinkhole. Or maybe a meteorite will hit earth and take us all out."

"Oh," Ernest says. He hopes Jane is just hungry and not a true misanthrope. His mother would cook him a meal of liver and onions when he was feeling blue. He twists his neck, anxious for someone to take their order.

"Yes?" asks the waiter, appearing at the table's edge.

Ernest watches Jane over the top of his menu. "Combo number two, please," she says, her eyes concealed behind the sunglasses like a rock star.

"Same." Ernest is nonchalant, going for a roadie vibe. He hasn't read the special menu the waiter brought them and has no idea what combo number two is, but he likes the idea of eating identical meals.

A few minutes later, the waiter brings their order, doused in neon sauce.

"Reminds me of being a kid," Ernest says, fumbling with the chopsticks. "My sister loved Chinese restaurants. She would stuff a chicken ball in each cheek, pretending to be a squirrel."

They leave a twenty on the table and walk toward the Cinesphere in silence, heading south. Remembering the fortune cookies they'd stuffed in their pockets, they stop to crack them open.

"Strange," says Jane, flipping her white scroll over. "Does yours have a fortune on it?"

"Good timber does not grow with ease," reads Ernest. "The stronger the wind, the stronger the trees."

"Uplifting," says Jane. "The trees are going to get chopped down anyway. What kind of fortune cookies are these?"

"Cheapies," says Ernest. "We should get a refund."

"Except they were free. Ernest?"

"Yes?"

"It's not true is it, what that guy was saying? The guy in the bar?"

"What do you think?" He searches her eyes. "Is something wrong with me?"

"Maybe." Jane's voice is barely audible. "But I like you."

"I like you too."

Meredith

Meredith smells industrial-grade cleaning agents as she opens the door. Ruth is inside, scrubbing the kitchen floor. Ruth has been trying to see her since the news broke around town but Meredith has been afraid to let anyone in.

Ruth drops the sponge. She rushes over to give Meredith a hug.

Meredith buries her face in Ruth's sweater. "Take me to Toronto."

"It's a big city, Merry."

"Help me find her."

Ruth sighs. "I did take the day off."

"I can see that. Why the hell are you cleaning my floor?"

"The floor's not the only thing that needs cleaning," Ruth says, pulling away to look at Meredith. "Why don't you have a shower? Then we'll check in with the cops and be on our way."

She steers her to the bathroom. "There's a fresh towel hanging on the back of the shower door."

Meredith blinks at her reflection under the fluorescent tube light. She can't remember the last time she's bathed. It must have been weeks ago, when she was still pretending she was okay, before she completely abdicated from her life. She strips and steps into the shower, letting the water blast her skin. She rubs the bar of soap between her palms as the steam clouds the glass. She lets herself feel hopeful that with Ruth's help, she'll find Jane.

Meredith runs her soapy hands over her tufty armpits and bristly legs. She'll clean herself up and go to Toronto, but she won't shave, she decides, arching her back. The water slips down her spine and off her tailbone. She'll keep a bit of wildness yet.

She brushes her teeth, remembering how Henry would call her "Lidless" with aggrieved affection when she'd forget to screw the toothpaste cap back on, the paste near the opening crusting. Tidiness had always been an effort for her. It was time she could have spent reading. She'd felt depressed by daily chores, tuned out when her mother had shown her how to do hospital corners. The daily habit of making beds that would only become unmade again seemed particularly pointless. Later, when she was married, she liked being alone in her car. She'd chuck her apple core on the ground when she was finished eating it, rubbing her sticky fingers all over the faux-leather seats.

She remembers putting Jane into her car seat when she was around three years old. After tightening the straps, Meredith had leaned in to give her daughter a kiss but Jane had pulled away.

Meredith's breath had caught in her throat. Her daughter had never done that before. Later, Jane would do the same to Henry, but it was still irksome that she'd been the one to be pushed away first.

Jane had grinned at her mother from her car seat that day, delighted by her newfound power, crumbs of kangaroo and hippopotamus clinging to the corners of her lips.

An hour later, Meredith is strapped into the passenger seat of Ruth's car. A garden gnome shares the back seat with a cooler of tuna fish sandwiches.

Ruth pushes a cassette tape into the deck. "Let's do this, Merry," she says determinedly. She turns the key in the ignition and the Tragically Hip's "At the Hundredth Meridian" fills the car. "Let's bring her home."

Jane

We stop in front of a vintage store. A pair of hot pink satin gloves drape over the gramophone on the table. Candy-coloured vintage shoes adorn the floor of the window display.

A steampunk teen looks up from behind the till when we enter. "Killer style," he says to Ernest.

Ernest smiles shyly then leads me to the source of the old-timey jazz. "A player piano," he whispers.

We watch the keys go up and down by themselves for a while before rifling through the racks. Fashion eras mingle. Ernest selects a black wool dress with a white Peter Pan collar and gives me a questioning look. "How about this?"

I shake my head. "Too scratchy."

He holds up a baby blue dress with a pink rosette belt next. "Looks to be about your size."

"Maybe if I was auditioning for one of the twins in *The Shining*."

Among the flower power miniskirts and dresses for tiny corseted waists, I spy a black mesh dress with an asymmetrical hem. I hold it up to my body and sigh. It's worthy of Siouxsie but too long for me. If Annie were here, I'd make her buy it. I return it reluctantly to the rack.

"You can't complain about this one," Ernest says, swishing a flapper dress in the air so it shimmers. "Try it on."

"Only if you try this." I trade him a navy satin opera coat.

"Although you probably have something similar at home."

When I come out of the change room, Ernest gasps. "You just need some pincurls. Actually you don't. You look perfect."

I curtsy. "You do too."

"Wait." He drapes a mink stole carefully around my neck. I jump when I see the dead paws and the taxidermied face nuzzling me in the mirror.

The shopkeeper laughs. "Suits you."

We leave without buying anything and turn onto a busy street. Cars and motorcycles rumble past, providing a bass line to the shouts and banter bursting from the apartment complexes lining the street. A family passes us, the parents dragging suitcases behind them. The youngest dabs boogers on her *My Little Pony* T-shirt and grins.

Something's been bothering me even though I've tried to shut it out. Some old gossip from Burr. Not the sleeping-with-the-dead-girl rumour that Annie and I used to spin yarns around. The other, more believable one.

I focus on Ernest's shambling shoes. "Can I ask you something?"

"Of course."

"On the streetcar… the sand, did it make you think of your sister? Didn't she drown?"

His eyes glisten but it's too late to turn back now. "What happened?"

He wets his lips, figuring out how to begin. We scan the traffic, then take the pedestrian bridge over the Gardiner Expressway. Cars are going faster than I've ever seen, hunks of metal hurtling themselves into the future.

Ernest takes a deep breath. There's relief in his face, as if he's been waiting a long time for someone to ask.

Ernest

Ernest had ignored Evelyn the first time she'd asked him to do it, continued carving in the sandcastle's bricks with his fingernail. She stood resolutely with her red bucket and plastic shovel, casting a shadow over him as she waited for an answer.

She tugged his arm until he lost his balance, an elbow crashing into the roof of the sandcastle he'd spent hours building.

Furious, he twisted his body to stare at her. "You ruin everything."

She held his eyes, unafraid. Then clambered into the hole she'd dug. "Bury me," she said again. This time it wasn't a question.

Farther down the beach, some kids had taken turns burying each other in the sand and now Evelyn wanted a go. He shielded his face with his hand, blocking out the rays that stabbed his eyes, blocking out his sister's expectant face too.

He toed the lump that used to be a castle and his throat constricted. *Fine!* He whipped a fistful of sand onto her legs. It felt good to make her disappear. When she was just a face on the beach, he stopped.

He squeezed his left eye closed, then his right one, alternating left, right, left, right, her face jumping from side to side. In one eye, she grinned mirthfully, in the other, she was blurry.

Left, right, left, right.

"I want to get out now," Evelyn said.

"No."

Ernest opened both eyes and saw hers well with tears.

Crocodile tears, he decided. For once, he wouldn't fall for it. It was time she learned a lesson. He turned his back and walked away.

He'd almost reached the main drag when her screams pulled him back. What if she wasn't just being dramatic? The pitch in her screams rose. He ran to where she was stuck in the hole and dug her out as fast as he could.

As soon as she was free, she was running, trampling over what was left of the sandcastle and racing to the shore, sand spraying off her body.

When Evelyn collapsed on the beach, he lifted her in his arms.

"I'm *dying* for ice cream," she said, laughing at her silly joke.

Ernest's money jingled in his pocket. He liked feeling the weight of what he'd earned pulling weeds. He was saving for the piano lessons his father refused to pay for, but Evelyn's face was still streaked with tears. Two ice cream cones wouldn't put him back much.

Of course the chocolate ice cream had tumbled onto Ernest's T-shirt in front of the girl with the silver tooth and of course the zit-pocked Gillespie Goons were there to witness it. Ralph Gillespie made a move for him as he disposed of the empty cone, squeezing his arm as if it were a wishbone.

"Stop it," said the girl with the silver tooth. Ralph's grip slackened and Ernest was able to slink toward the door, where Evelyn was waiting with her strawberry ice cream cone.

He had no idea why Silver Tooth had rescued him from the Gillespies. He stared at her.

Evelyn ate her ice cream furtively. "Let's go back to the beach," she whispered between licks.

The Goons were speaking to Silver Tooth but she pushed them away. "Hey Ernest, wait," she said, her canine glinting with special powers. She nodded at Evelyn and stepped between them, synching her step to Ernest's. The Goons followed wordlessly at a safe distance.

Ernest wondered what was happening and how Silver Tooth had known his name.

What was it that mesmerized Ernest about the gulls that day? Was it the wings dipped in black? The soft bellies? Or how they'd soared, barely flapping?

Maybe it wasn't the gulls at all, but Silver Tooth and the hand-rolled cigarette the Goons passed to him. "No hard feelings, eh?"

He'd never smoked a cigarette before. He thought skunky cabbage was how tobacco tasted.

Evelyn scowled and dug a big hole in the sand. She mouthed, "You're dead," and drew her finger ominously across her neck.

Ernest passed the cigarette back and forth with Silver Tooth. Was he dreaming?

Silver Tooth was thirteen and he was eleven which dictated that even if he was incredibly cool, she would still not go anywhere near him, especially not somewhere where they could be seen together (unless they were related, but even then...). No, in real life, he'd be hacking up his lungs like the baby-faced loser he was while she strode by in her Daisy Dukes, felling square-jawed high schoolers with each step. She didn't even need that mystical fang. She could have passed for sixteen, easy. And she was pretty.

Ernest tried to think of something casual to say. "I like your silver tooth," he managed.

"It's made of mercury, tin, copper and silver, actually. I can pick up radio signals with it," she said, running her tongue over it.

It sounded like a tall tale but Ernest leaned in anyway. After a few seconds of intense concentration, he sensed a buzzing. Cheers and chatter and radio crackle.

"I guess if this thing comes up short, he can field it," said the tooth in a manly voice.

"Thomas keeps it. Thomas has still got it. Oh my God. Fifty. Forty-five. Forty. There he goes! Thirty. No one's left to stop him!"

The tooth cheered wildly for a few seconds then fell silent.

"Whoa," Ernest breathed. "That's something."

She blinked at him. "No one but me can hear it," she said.

"Oh," said Ernest. "I feel kind of funny."

"Lie down," said Silver Tooth. "Take a nap." She stretched out her tanned legs and adjusted her short shorts.

Ernest's eyelids fluttered. He wondered what Silver Tooth was whispering to the Goons.

The last thing he saw before he fell asleep was a flock of sea-gulls flying overhead, their webbed yellow feet hanging stiffly, like plastic.

He came to as Silver Tooth was leaving. He lay there with his melted legs, watching her recede. After she was gone, he kept watching that vacated bit of sky. His tongue a wool sock.

He wondered when the Goons had left, and why they'd decided to be kind to him. Wondered if hand-rolled cigarettes had as much magic as radio-signal teeth.

He propped himself up on his elbows. People left the beach, going home to put on their regular clothes and have dinner. Eve-lyn ran in and out of his vision in her striped bathing suit, scoop-ing sand in one place and dumping it out in another.

He still felt woozy. The trees shook their hair at him and the sun sparked on the water and he was amazed by how alive it all was. He tingled.

His pockets felt light and when he reached inside he realized the money he'd been saving was missing.

He saw the red shovel and the overturned bucket a few feet in front of him.

He saw his sister thrashing in the water. Then just her fingertips.

Meredith

Meredith looks out the car window as Ruth speeds through the outskirts of London. Despite the name, there was an American feel to this city, with its football games and fraternities and distrust of big government. At summer parties held in the wealthier enclaves where Henry's colleagues lived, Meredith approached the shimmering women gathered around their swimming pools and felt as though she'd entered her television set.

Meredith's favourite part of parties was leaving them. The mouthfeel of late summer darkness as she and Henry exited their car and climbed the stairs to their front door. The grasshoppers rubbing their hind legs against the edge of their wings. The frogs blowing their bubble gum throats in the trees.

They would dismiss the babysitter early and sneak into their daughter's room to watch her sleep, before heading to the living room for *Seinfeld* reruns. They laughed when George shouted and Elaine rolled her eyes and Kramer fell down. Meredith was thrilled by the laugh track too. The strangers giggling among them, unseen.

The sound of canned laughter fills the car, waking Meredith from her reverie.

"Wow, tough crowd," Ruth says, smiling at her in the rearview mirror.

"I wasn't listening."

"It's supposed to be comedy. It's actually funny if you pay attention. Some hotshot on the New York circuit."

Meredith shivers. "That laughter."

"You have a problem with the laughter?"

"Laugh tracks were taped in the 1950s and haven't been updated."

"So?"

"So what you're hearing is a bunch of dead people laughing at this guy's jokes."

"They might not all be dead."

Meredith tilts her head, considering. "Probably some middle-aged people and elderly people," she concedes. "But there are definitely dead guys laughing with them."

Ruth shudders and turns the dial to a golden oldies channel. The sha-la-las and doo-wops of deceased pop stars fill the car. Ruth is oblivious to the irony, singing along, until chugging organ funk fills the car. The song is unmistakable.

"I like 'Spirit in the Sky,'" protests Meredith as Ruth's finger hovers over the scan button.

Ruth pushes it anyway. She adjusts the volume. "What if it's true? What if Jane is in some sort of relationship with Ernest?"

"I don't want to talk about it," Meredith manages. She knew it was her fault Jane had left.

The radio cycles through its frequencies, stopping to play whatever snatch of song, commercial or news bulletin it finds between the static. Meredith presses her head against the window, desperate to break out.

Jane

Lake Ontario stretches before us. Ernest watches the water intently, as if he's scanning the surface for a small hand that needs saving.

The wind picks up, blowing me against him. Ernest's body feels fragile, like his skeleton is made of bird bones. The underside of the clouds glow pink.

"I wish I could have saved her," he says into my hair.

"I wish I could have saved Dad too."

Ernest's breath is warm on my scalp. "Where were you when it happened?"

"At school. Mom saw his spirit leave his body and there was nothing anyone could do."

"I read about this man in the newspaper. The paramedics restarted his heart, but they couldn't fix his brain. The hospital hooked his body to a machine for years. A decade even."

"So I should be grateful to remember him at the peak of his life? I hate when people say stuff like that. He would have wanted to say goodbye. To say something we could have held on to."

Ernest is quiet. We stand there for a while, sharing what's left of the sun on this bit of beach. In the distance, the highway hums with people making their way to their families, or to nightclubs and night shifts.

I kick off my loafers and help Ernest remove his socks and shoes. His feet glow coldly, the knuckles of his big toes poking out.

I stand. The lake looks different now the sun is down, the water drained of colour.

"Jane?"

"What?"

"Is it possible your Dad was saying those things all along?"

"What things?"

"The things to hold on to?"

I smile at him through the darkness.

He bends over. "Let's collect some sticks."

"What for?"

"The birthday party."

Ernest makes the kind of sense a dream makes when you're asleep and you go along with it because you have to, and because you want to, too.

I stash the sticks I find in my hitched-up skirt. When we have the right number, we set them down in a pile. I take one and draw a huge circle, then a small circle within. We push the other sticks into the sand between them, counting out loud. Forty-three candles and a Harvey Wallbanger birthday cake.

When we inspected sand in science class last year, Annie and I were surprised that the grains were different shapes and colours, made of crushed quartz and bits of seashells. I thought it'd be cool to mix the sand with the lavender Hard Candy polish we'd bought together at the mall, encrusting our nails with secret, microscopic beauty. Annie said our hands would look dirty.

Ernest reaches into his pocket and gives me a pack of matches. "Ready?" he asks. If Dad were alive, Mom and I would be singing to him in the dark.

I wonder what Mom will do tomorrow. Will she celebrate Dad's birthday alone?

I set the sticks alight. We sing "Happy Birthday" and the flames lick the sticks until the wind snuffs the last one out.

"Close your eyes. Make a wish," Ernest says.

I'm not sure if he's addressing my dead father or me. Behind us, the lake ripples with unseen currents.

I sleepwalk toward him and grasp his wrists. I imagine the skull under his face. The holes behind his eyes. Death feels closer when I'm with him. As if a flash of lightning could illuminate the skeletons under our skins.

I pull him toward me, pressing my mouth to his.

Ernest pushes me away, losing his balance and falling backwards.

My eyes burn. Wasn't that what he wanted?

His fingers push up through the sand. After a moment, I grab his hands and lean back on my heels, pulling with all my weight until he's back on his feet.

He coughs as I brush grains off his face.

"Jane—"

"You don't need to say it."

I'm glad it's night and he can't see my cheeks redden with shame.

Meredith

As they approach Toronto, Meredith concentrates on where Jane might be. She remembers how Henry used to visualize victory before his wrestling matches and how he began to win and win. She thinks about what she wants to happen. She conjures Jane watching baseball at the SkyDome. A memory from when Henry was alive. She asks Ruth to drive there now.

They'd gone a couple of summers ago, after Henry's colleague had given them free tickets to a Blue Jays game. The Jays were on a winning streak and the SkyDome had rippled with waves. They'd eaten hot dogs striped with ketchup and mustard, and drank overpriced beer out of plastic cups, tearing the tags off their new blue caps and pulling them over their ears. It was Meredith and Jane's first ball game.

The players were casual, it seemed to Meredith, standing around and chatting. When they managed to hit the ball, half the time they didn't run very fast. Henry laughed when she told him her impressions, her concern the players weren't trying hard enough.

"It's an endurance test for the players," he'd explained good-naturedly. "They play 162 games in about 180 days and get no more than three days off a month. Sure, they conserve their energy, but they're definitely athletes."

"They only come to bat a few times," said Jane. "Can't they sprint if they hit something?"

"But if they hit a fly ball, there's a 99 percent chance it will result in someone catching the ball."

"The stakes aren't high enough," persisted Meredith. "There's no, what do you call it—"

"Sudden death?"

"Yeah, exactly. Even if they lose, they still play the same team a few more times, right?"

"The leisurely pace is part of the pleasure. Allows you time to conduct your own strategy analysis internally or—"

"Strategy analysis?" Jane slurped her Coke. "You're really selling the fun factor."

"Okay, okay." Henry lifted his hands in mock defence. "There's also the park-like setting. And the one-on-one conflict between pitcher and batter. It's a team sport, but each game is like a series of one-on-one interactions."

They looked at him doubtfully before returning their attention to the diamond. Meredith tried to be open-minded the rest of the game but felt by the end of it that baseball lacked the Shakespearean drama of Henry's wrestling bouts, or the singles tennis matches on TV.

That was their old life. In her new life, Meredith doesn't sit in front of the TV. She unplugged it, just to be safe. She was afraid of the pixels arranging themselves into her daughter's face.

Recently, she's been afraid of Henry's face appearing too, in the dormant machine. What would he say to her now?

As they approach the turtle-shell dome, Meredith's head pounds. Over fifty thousand people can fit in the stadium— even if Jane was there, how on earth would they find her? They don't even have tickets.

The streets are quieter than Meredith expects. They find a parking spot easily. When they arrive at the entrance, the

SkyDome is closed, a sign detailing an ongoing Major League Baseball strike on the door.

Ruth rubs her face. "We should find somewhere to sleep."

As they leave the empty stadium behind, Meredith closes her eyes. She imagines Jane zooming underground on a subway seat, cheek pressed against the glass. Or swaying in an all-ages club, her face glistening under roving polka dots of light.

She sees her floating on her back in Lake Ontario at night. Kicking her legs slowly as she names the constellations. Unlike in Jane's bedroom, the stars in Meredith's vision are real, unpeeling.

Burr

The townspeople put up *Missing Child* posters all over Burr and downtown London. They tape Jane's face onto bus stops and pay phones, over rewards for missing pets.

A London anchorwoman records an interview with Annie.

"She was my best friend, but we grew apart."

"What happened?"

Mascara runs down Annie's face in black rivulets. "She changed."

"How?"

"She pulled away. From me. From school."

"If you could tell her something now, what would it be?"

"Jane," she says, voice breaking, "come home."

Citizens swap rumours and theories. It doesn't end well for a young girl who doesn't play by the town's rules, or for any kind of female runaway. Read a newspaper. Turn on the TV.

It ends with a hole dug hastily with a shovel. Body parts in a freezer, wrapped in butcher paper. A dredged pond.

If not now, it ends this way later.

They imagine Jane lit up by a stranger's headlights, raising her thumb. Turning into air.

Jane

When I wake up on the beach next to Ernest, I think of the schoolyard rumour about him sleeping with his eyes open and the voices of my classmates fill my head. I remember the swoosh of dodgeballs narrowly missing my legs, and the smell of Annie's sweat as she whipped the ball at the opposing team, whooping when she hit them. I feel a pang of missing her and wonder if she's gone to third base with Andrew yet, if she would even tell me now, or if our friendship is gone for good, buried in the forest with our orphan games.

"Penny for your thoughts," Ernest says.

"Do you really sleep with your eyes open?"

Ernest smiles. "What do you think?"

"Everyone says you do. Well, kids at my school, anyway."

"I try. To keep my eyes open, I mean. I like to watch the curtains in my room at night. The light changing. I can dream and watch at the same time."

"Did you watch me last night?"

"Of course."

"What was I dreaming of?"

"You can't remember?"

"Nope."

"I can't say for sure."

"Guess."

"You were deep-sea diving."

"For what?"

"Pearls. But the pearls turned out to be baby teeth."

"Creepy."

Ernest laughs. "People often dream of teeth, you know."

"If you say so."

Mom keeps my baby teeth in a black lacquered box on her dresser. I used to run them one at a time along my arm when she was getting ready to go out, feeling the little ridges that used to crush peas and pieces of chicken. It was hard to imagine they had once been a part of me. When I watched Mom change, I'd find myself staring at the crinkly skin of her belly. It was strange to think I used to swim inside of her.

Now my teeth are big and straight and a little worn, probably because I grind my teeth like Dad. Ernest's teeth are small and tea coloured, some steeped longer than others. One of the bottom ones is twisted, as if it was screwed on too loose or too tight.

"I like your teeth," I tell him.

"Even though they're not dentures?"

"I always knew they were real," I admit.

We get up and stroll along the fringes of the lake. In the distance, the trapped moon of the Cinesphere beckons. Ernest buys us a large popcorn and IMAX tickets to watch *Africa: The Serengeti* inside. I lie back in the half-filled theatre and try not to think about the kiss while elephants trumpet and mohawked zebras gallop across the eighty-foot-wide screen.

We walk north alongside the grounds of Medieval Times, past a curly-haired off-duty knight eating a banana and a poster of a jouster on a rearing white horse. I try to stay calm, shutting up the voice that says it's Mom I should be spending Dad's birthday with.

We suck on grape popsicles as we wander, our tongues purpling under the sun. We pass an indie record shop and I think of Dad. I hope he forgives me for being embarrassed by him in front of my first crush, who worked at Sunrise Records in London's Masonville Mall.

It was in the fall of seventh grade. Dad and I had gone to Masonville one Saturday to shop. I'd spent a lot of time getting ready that morning trying to look like I'd spent no time. I used Mom's eyeliner then smeared most of it off, for that slept-in look. I put Dad's gel in my hair to convey the impression it hadn't been washed in days. I stayed up extra late the night before reading Edgar Allan Poe by flashlight so I'd appear extra haunted.

"Noah." I whispered his name to the Rice Krispies in my bowl and they popped and crackled it back to me.

Dad and I split in front of Jean Machine and agreed to meet back there in an hour. Noah didn't look up when I entered Sunrise alone. I gazed at the black eyelashes fringing his blue eyes. His hair was messy and imperfect, like he'd cut it himself, and he was wearing his usual uniform: faded Nirvana T-shirt, ripped jeans, black eyeliner. I flipped through the racks of alternative CDs and plucked at the seam of my flannel shirt until I remembered what I'd told Dad I'd come to buy. I didn't have much time to make Noah fall for me. I cleared my throat, holding up PJ Harvey's *Rid of Me*.

"Do you have *4-Track Demos*?"

"Don't think so, but that's a heavy album you've got right there."

"Yeah, but Albini drowned her vocals. *Demos*, PJ produced on her own."

I'd impressed him. "Did she?"

This was going better than expected. In my fantasy, we were halfway to a date at Orange Julius on his lunch break. To sharing Manchu Wok on an orange plastic tray. To starting our own band. I guessed he was the bassist type (quietly hot with nice biceps and a medium-large ego), but if he had front-man ambitions we could get a second microphone and sing some grungy duets together.

"Yes." I held his gaze even though I was blushing. Noah combed his greasy hair with his fingers. The record store spun.

"Get your PJ Jammies CD, Jane?" Dad's voice boomed.

"Harvey, Dad. It's Harvey," I hissed, as Noah laughed. I glared at my father. "We were *supposed* to meet at Jean Machine."

"Thought it made sense to meet here." He rubbed my shoulder and turned to Noah. "Hey man," he said. "Got Enya's latest in stock?"

Noah gestured to the bestsellers display rack.

"That's your Dad?" He squinted.

I nodded bleakly.

The next time I saw Noah he was making out with Althea against a dumpster by the mall's back entrance and I wondered if it was one of the ones Dad searched in for my dead body when I was little.

It took me forever to get over it. Annie pointed out all we'd had was a boring conversation and it was Noah's job to talk to people and sell CDs. I haven't crushed on anyone at school. I don't want to stick my tongue down some dumb jock's throat, unlike Annie.

I think of how I'd wished in the record store that Dad didn't belong to me.

I knew I loved him. I didn't know how much.

Meredith

Meredith wakes to the mini-fridge hum of the hotel room Ruth found for them last night. She turns her face to gaze through the thin curtains. The city is not yet light.

She concentrates on where Jane might be, but the images of the subway car and the club could be anywhere in Toronto and she can't bear to think about her daughter floating in the lake.

Instead, she thinks of the last time they were together in Toronto. She and Henry had taken Jane and Annie to see Tori Amos perform at the University of Toronto's Convocation Hall.

Tori was a bit dramatic for Henry's taste, but Meredith had been mesmerized by her performance. It felt, despite the crowd, as though Meredith were privy to an experience that was private. Sacred, even. The musician channelling something otherworldly as she writhed on the piano bench. Meredith's skin pricked with heat.

Meredith knows the venue is close to where they're staying. She'd glimpsed the campus last night from the car window as they'd sped by.

A few hours later, Meredith and Ruth enter the rotunda with its turquoise copper-clad dome. Inside, volunteers are setting up for an Arctic botany conference. A young woman asks for their names and apologizes: they don't seem to be on the list. Meredith doesn't tell her that they're not academics. She sticks on the name tag the volunteer gives her, absentmindedly leaving it blank.

"You said this was a music venue," murmurs Ruth.

Other than the majestic pipe organ, the space feels completely different than when Meredith was here last. Under happier circumstances, she'd appreciate the architecture in the daylight, would feel soothed by the building's radial design.

Graduations are held here in the spring. Henry will never see Jane wearing an academic cap. Will she?

She lifts her wet eyes to the oculus in the ceiling. What would Henry do if he were here?

Her husband would surely find her current search plan fanciful, but he wasn't as systematic as he seemed. He had also been led by feelings, which bordered on irrational at times. She remembers when Jane went missing at the mall and she caught him opening a garbage bin.

Could Henry be with her right now, helping her look for Jane again?

If you're here and you know anything, she dares the large glass eye, *give me a goddamn sign.*

Jane

My body feels kinked from another night of sleeping outdoors. I rub my neck as we wait for the orange outline of a hand to turn into a white walker. We're finally on our way to the haunted house.

Burr has no traffic lights. Just red stop signs, including a couple of extra-big ones at the intersection where cars have crashed over the years.

I feel a pang for Burr's insect rhythms and deep dark, for the lonely high beams speeding through. I want Annie to overhear all the adventures I've been up to. I want her jealous. If she was serious about leaving Burr, if she cared about me, wouldn't she have come?

Parents are probably watching their kids extra closely now. And it's possible someone is here, trying to find me. Possibly a small team. Could I really expect Mom not to search for me?

"Ernest—"

He turns.

"I bet they're looking for us. I shouldn't have called Mom."

"What can they do?"

"They'll take us back."

"I don't mind Burr when I'm with you," Ernest says, gripping my hand as we cross the street.

"They won't understand."

His face falters. "But I haven't done anything wrong."

"I don't know if that matters."

The city bustles around us, unconcerned about our disappearance from Burr and our date with the dead. A man in a suit passes us hurriedly, licking frozen yogurt off a tiny plastic spoon. Heavy strollers transport sleeping babies. A teenager blows smoke rings into her boyfriend's face.

"Do you think a ghost will show up?" I ask Ernest, as we step gingerly into bright beams of sun.

My question surprises him. "Isn't that what we're paying for?"

"Will we recognize who it is?"

"You mean, will the ghost be someone we know?"

"Like Evelyn."

"Or your father." A sideways look. "Are you nervous?"

"A bit."

"Me too."

We reach an intersection at the corner of a leafy park. Teenage boys sit on top of a set of monkey bars, pretending to be bored. One locks eyes with me. His friends laugh when he blows me a kiss.

"We're supposed to turn somewhere around here," I say, ignoring the boys and scanning the street signs. "Ernest, can you pass the map?"

Ernest stares at his hands, then rifles through his pockets. "Shoot," he says anxiously.

"We could retrace our steps in case it blew out of your pocket." The boys are sitting under the monkey bars now, passing a joint around. "Or," I say, dubious, "we could ask them."

A black and white cat leaps out from a bush and rubs against our ankles before strutting ahead of us.

"Follow her," Ernest says with conviction.

I raise my eyebrow but Ernest just gestures to follow the black tail. I shake my head as we turn the corner, trailing the trotting paws.

Our cat leader reminds me of Groucho and I wish I could scratch him under his chin and kiss his damp black nose. I shouldn't have left him alone with Mom. I vow to pay more attention to him when I return and promise to throw the catnip mouse for at least twenty-five minutes every day to make up for it. I try not to think about what else I'll have to face.

Meredith

As they leave the campus, Meredith is distraught. She can't feel Henry's presence at all. It was a stupid idea to come here. What the hell should she and Ruth do now?

Her friend doesn't ask where to go next. She just drives. They head south, passing a shelter, old men sharing smokes outside.

Ruth smacks the steering wheel with her hand when she notices the needle of the fuel gauge bobbing on empty. She parks on a lively street. While Ruth ducks into a convenience store to ask where the nearest gas station is, Meredith gets out and leans against the car. She notices a flashing neon palm across the street.

She waits for a gap in the traffic and darts to the other side, stepping over the trash littering the sidewalk. A woman around her age with dyed-red hair and gold hoop earrings ushers her in. Meredith follows her through a bead curtain, into a back room. The walls are deep purple and hung with abstract art. Meredith wonders if the psychic did them herself.

"Marina," says the psychic, shaking her hand.

"Meredith. How much is a reading?'

"It depends. You pay me, but I actually work for the spirits." She smiles. "They're the ones who sent you here. They're the ones sending the messages. But generally speaking, it's twenty dollars per half-hour."

They settle into facing office armchairs, a small table between them. Marina reclines in front of a painting. Yellow brushstrokes emanate from her head.

"You've suffered a great shock," the psychic says, her palms facing upward. "You've lost someone dear to you." Her brow furrows. "Perhaps more than one."

Tears stream down Meredith's face.

"Your family is in jeopardy." The psychic opens her eyes. "But I can help."

"How?"

"I can connect with the other side. It's right on top of us." She watches Meredith take a tissue from the box on the table and blow her nose. "Think of that tissue you're holding. The membrane between their world and ours is that thin."

"The dead are right here, with us?"

"I read palms. But sometimes, like with you, I don't need to. The spirit just comes through."

"He's here? Now?"

The psychic nods. "I'm receiving a message. From a man. A little older."

"My husband."

"Yes. He wants to tell you he's okay. That you were a wonderful wife. He wants you to know that he loves you."

"And where is my daughter?" Meredith asks, panic-stricken. "Is she with him?"

The front door bangs open. Ruth pushes through the bead curtain and gives Meredith an exasperated look.

"I'm in the middle of something."

"Let's go," Ruth hisses, regarding Marina with suspicion.

The psychic looks weary. Is she also carrying a burden, caused by her extrasensory perception? Or is it the toll of being regularly treated with scorn?

She speaks quietly to Meredith: "It's your life, isn't it? What do you want to do?"

"I'm sorry," Meredith says, handing her a twenty with a shaking hand. "I'm going to talk to my friend."

"Listen to your intuition," Marina says, tucking the money in her pocket. "We're all mediums. We all have gifts."

"She knew what was going on," Meredith protests, after Ruth practically shoves her out the door. "She could tell I've suffered a great loss."

"It's called a cold reading," Ruth says. "Anyone looking at you could tell that."

Ernest

The cat twitches her whiskered nose at him. She looks up, so Ernest does too. A mackerel sky, the clouds rippling like scales.

Evelyn's near. Did she send the cat to help them? He's still gazing at the sky when Jane tugs him across the road.

They follow the cat along the street, past pawnshops and galleries and an appliance centre done up as a Japanese temple, dusty karate photos hung between refrigerators.

On the edge of a park where old men play cards and drink beer, the cat darts across the street. Ernest and Jane follow in close pursuit. Cars honk and swerve.

Where did the cat go? Ernest spins around until he's dizzy. She's not at the house with the boarded-up windows, or in the back of the beat-up truck idling on the corner.

Ah, there she is! Sitting on the doorstep of a Victorian choked with ivy, grooming her coat. Ernest quickens his pace, pulling Jane with him. The cat pauses, mid-lick, as they approach.

"Wait a sec—" Jane's eyes flit from the number peeking out of the leaves to the address in the newspaper clipping. "This is it," she says incredulously. "How—?"

Ernest gives her his most enigmatic look. He wishes he was still wearing the opera coat.

He consults his pocket watch. They are early, even.

"Magical cat," Jane whispers into the feline's fur, stroking her cheeks until she purrs.

The air smells faintly of Evelyn's breath—a mixture of gummy bears and sour milk. Ernest touches a crumbling brick.

Jane lifts the cat into her arms and cranes her head to take in the missing roof tiles. "Fallen on hard times."

"Who hasn't?"

She gives him a death stare. "Except for you," he says. "You don't need to shower."

"People in grunge bands go weeks without bathing."

They contemplate the house for a moment. Ernest tilts his head toward the oak door. "Well," he says, "I'm ready when you are."

Jane releases the cat. She feels for the doorbell under the ivy. They jump as it rings somewhere deep within.

Jane

It smells like smoke and wax, old books and offerings. Candles flicker, casting the blacked-out foyer in a pale, unsteady light. A stuffed owl stares at us from his perch in the corner. The wallpaper is green and blue, harebells and fronds in various states of unfurling.

A candle snuffs out. Then another. Tendrils of smoke drift toward the tin ceiling.

I shiver.

"This house has its own weather system." Ernest rubs his arms.

It's true. The wind whistles in our ears and breathes down our backs, ruffling our clothes and the owl's feathers.

"No matter what happens," Ernest whispers, "I'm here."

I nod, my heart beating in my ears.

I try to project grunge-rocker energy but I have a feeling I'm just grimy. We washed up in a coffee shop restroom this morning but it didn't do much good. I comb my fingers through my hair and sand falls out.

A woman in a flowing cream dress and smoky eyeshadow appears in the archway. She wears a crisp bob and a black headband slung low across her forehead. It's like she's time-travelled from some faraway era, from before Ernest was born.

"I'm Brenda," she says.

The woman doesn't resemble a Brenda. More of a Cassandra. Or an Isadora.

The alleged Brenda smiles. "Come in," she says serenely.

We follow her down a yellow-tiled corridor until we reach a closed door. Brenda stops and presses her ear against it before gently turning the knob. She ushers us into an emerald parlour with a stone fireplace and a wrought-iron chandelier.

Brenda gestures to a row of velvet seats. "Please make yourselves comfortable," she says. "The others should be here shortly."

A tall old-fashioned cabinet sits on a sawhorse at the front of the room, doors open. Other than the seats and a wooden table in the corner, it's the only piece of furniture in the room.

As soon as Brenda leaves, Ernest and I approach the cabinet. I lean my head back to take in the fancy carvings at the top: cresting waves with a seashell in the centre. There aren't any drawers inside. No pole to hang coats from. There's a vertical divider creating two compartments. I stare at the empty spaces and try not to think of Dad and his closet, of everything gone missing.

I notice a slab of wood set up like a bench, as if this cabinet were a place to hang out in. I'm reminded of the line in the newspaper ad about the medium and his assistant confining themselves so we don't get suspicious and the setup starts to make sense.

"This must be where Drood conjures the ghost with his assistant," I tell Ernest.

Ernest pokes his head into the cabinet, his voice echoing inside the cavity. "Why does he crawl in here to do it?"

"So we know they're not impersonating the spirit."

"We're supposed to lock them inside so they can't get out?"

"Either that or he doesn't want us to see what he's really doing during the séance."

Ernest searches my face. "This could be some kind of act?"

I open and close the cabinet doors. "I'm just scared to get my hopes up."

"I'm not a carpenter," Ernest says, running his fingers along the interior, "but it seems like a normal cabinet me."

I peer at the underside, kneeling beside the sawhorse, checking for trap doors.

"Any signs of skullduggery?" inquires a sweetly authoritative voice. British accent, more folksy than the ones in Merchant Ivory movies. I scramble to my feet and come face to face with a woman with two long silver braids and a high-collared blue dress with a row of buttons down the front.

"No need to be embarrassed," says the woman, amused. "I'm Eloise." With her upturned nose and bosomy body, she's beautiful in a fairy godmother kind of way. "There have, and always will be, skeptics…"

"I, uh, dropped something."

"Did you find it?"

My cheeks flush. "Not yet."

Ernest helps the rose-scented lady to a seat. "Thank you, dear," she says, daintily adjusting the hem of her dress over her knees. She pulls needles out of her purse and begins to pearl and knit. "You'll be persuaded after the séance," she says, needles clacking. "I myself am a fifth-generation spiritualist."

Ernest watches her movements closely. "I'm a lefty too," he says. "They tied my left arm behind me so I wouldn't be able to write with it at school."

"They thwacked my left hand with a ruler, made me sit on it at lunch."

"Why?" I ask, confused.

"Sign of the devil," Ernest says.

I can't believe there are people alive who experienced these things in the olden days.

Aside from a few comments about growing up in a big family on a farm with chickens and horses, Dad hardly told me anything about his childhood. Why didn't I find out when he was alive? Why didn't I beg to meet his family? Now that he's dead I'll never be able to ask him.

A dozen or so people trickle in. I gaze at a PJ Harvey lookalike in a leopard slip. She catches my eye and comes over, introducing herself as Mona.

"I'm a death doula," she says, knotting her glossy black hair into a loose bun with her fingers. "Part of the death positive movement. And my brother Allan here," she points at a stocky guy in a baseball cap muscling his way over to our group, "is in death tech."

Ernest and I look at each other.

"Green burials mostly," adds Allan, shaking our hands. "My company's doing R & D into biodegradable urns, aquamation, recomposition. Stuff like that."

"What's a death doula?" I ask, committing to memory the shade of her red lips (exactly midway between blood and tomato).

"I actually prefer the term thanadoula," she says. "Thana comes from the Ancient Greek word *thanatos,* meaning death. And *doula* means servant." She's about to say more when Brenda reappears, striking a triangle with a metal wand to get our attention.

We hold our breath in the ringing air. The footsteps in the corridor come closer. A man enters the room dressed in a white tunic and slacks. A photograph of my father, taken when I was a toddler, come to life. Faded blue eyes, big nose and a shock of blond hair, longer than I remember it. My father from ten years ago, striding toward me on bare feet.

The medium straightens and before my eyes becomes someone else, someone two inches taller than my father.

"Welcome," he says, in an unexpectedly nasally voice.

His frame is different. Lankier.

His eyes are more grey than blue and spark like television snow. He leans in, smelling like a mix of incense and hairspray. "Are you okay?"

I thought I'd given up trying to find Dad in crowds. The séance hasn't even started yet and it's the best chance I have of him showing up. So why am I upset now, on the verge of finding him?

He reaches out to shake my hand. "Call me Alabaster."

"Jane."

He stares into my eyes and doesn't release my hand. "There's someone you wish to contact."

I nod.

"Hmm," Alabaster says, tilting his head and staring into the distance as if he were receiving information about Dad from an invisible walkie-talkie. "I see." Then to me, he says, "A family member?"

"My dad," I say, voice catching in my throat.

He gazes into the distance, stroking his chin.

"He's a wrestler. With arms like this—" My fingers trace invisible muscles above my arm. "His name is Henry."

He squeezes my fingers. "You'll recognize him if he comes."

I motion to Ernest to meet the medium with me but he doesn't budge, just cowers against the green wall as though he wishes it would swallow him up.

"Wait—" I say. "My friend is shy but there's someone he wants to contact too."

Alabaster follows my gaze across the room.

"His little sister," I explain. "Her name is Evelyn. She drowned a long time ago."

"Unfinished business," Alabaster muses, sizing Ernest up.

"She's not at rest."

"Some spirits aren't aware their body is dead," Alabaster says sympathetically. "They need to be guided toward that realization."

"How?"

"A spirit rescue. It's our bread and butter."

I swallow, remembering when Annie's mom briefly rekindled her Catholic roots and dragged us to church one time. "Like a Eucharist kind of thing?"

Alabaster looks amused. "I just meant we do spirit rescues a lot."

Did Dad immediately know he was dead, and if he did, how did he take it? He believed in the circle of life when it came to animals and other people. Mom said he was hoping to live forever, or at least outlast the other men his age.

"Let us know if you'd like to set one up." He releases me and glides to the next person.

As I squint at the medium's receding back, I can't believe Ernest and I pulled it off. We escaped Burr and made it to the next best thing to New York City. And now we're in a haunted house with twenty or so other people who refuse to move on with their lives and a man that looks like Dad, only younger and weirdly bright.

Ernest shambles over as soon as I'm alone. I thought he would feel excited to be in the presence of the man who may be able to beckon his dead sister's spirit and bring her back to him. But instead he seems threatened by the way the medium moves through the room. Cracking jokes, making each guest feel special as they enter his orbit. I think of Ernest's old-timey outfits and the way he juggled oranges for me on the train. Does he wish he had magical powers like Alabaster?

Before I can tell him what the medium said, Brenda strikes her triangle. "The séance is about to commence," she says.

I sit beside Ernest and Allan takes the seat on the other side of me, scrutinizing Alabaster Drood's every move. If I didn't already know he was a paranormal investigator, I'd think Allan was a skeptic himself. He pulls something that kind of looks like a Walkman out of his briefcase and hides it in his lap.

Alabaster strides to the front of the room. He opens his arms wide, a friendly blond vampire who wants to embrace us all in one big, bloody hug. Maybe it's because we're sitting down but he looks gigantic. As if he's been growing off our energy this whole time.

"The time has come," he declares, "to summon the spirits."

Meredith

Around the corner from the fortune teller's shop, a muscular man races down the sidewalk. He's clad in high-tech athletic wear, Discman in hand and headphones in his ears. His stubbled face is stern with concentration. He cuts a straight line through Meredith and Ruth as if he doesn't see them. They jump out of his way.

"Watch where you're going!" shouts Ruth.

Meredith used to run with Henry. She misses the sweat and grunt of it. Those airborne seconds before her feet hit the ground when her body felt light and ageless. The wild lilac she carried in her hands. In the spring they'd break off branches as they got close to the house and put them in jam jars on their bedside tables. Filling their lungs with the almost too-sweet scent before the flowers drooped and browned. She feels guilty for the extravagance. How quickly they had needed to be thrown out.

He'd wear the same pair of grey Zellers sweatpants on their runs and over the years they became holey and the elastic band lost its snap. Meredith pointedly bought Henry new ones from Roots for Christmas but he refused to wear them.

She was embarrassed by the way he looked in his sweatpants and wished he'd been wearing something different the last time they went running together. He hadn't looked like her husband when the paramedics came, or like a former world-class wrestler. He looked like some other middle-aged man in saggy sweats who'd dropped dead beside her on the road.

She didn't understand why she was still alive, or how her own breath kept going in and out. A car came and she stood in its way and screamed and swung her arms until it stopped. She doesn't remember her neighbours getting out of the car, or what they'd said. She does remember the wife crouching beside Henry and pressing her coral lips on his.

Henry was dead before he hit the ground. She'd seen the life slip out of his eyes. But Meredith still wishes she'd known CPR, that she'd been the one to try.

Ernest

Ernest claps uncertainly when the room applauds. Like Jane, he's a little afraid. The visions he's had of Evelyn have always been private ones. He's not sure he's ready to share her spirit with a crowd.

"I'm sensing a lot of energy in here," Alabaster shouts. "Powerful energy. Positive energy. And I'll tell you what. I'm in the mood for something different. Shall we do things a little differently today?"

The audience cheers.

"I'll take that as a yes." Alabaster beams. "Okay Brenda. Before we move on to the grand finale, let's pay homage to our forefathers with a dark séance."

"What's that?" Ernest quietly asks Allan.

"A pre-spirit cabinet technique," he explains in a rapid-fire whisper, "in which the mediums are bound and the manifestations take place in total darkness."

Brenda and Alabaster blow dust off something before lifting it out of the shadows and into the centre of the room. At first Ernest mistakes the long wooden table for a coffin.

"May I have a volunteer?" Brenda calls out.

Ernest looks down. He hated being called on in class.

"What exactly are we volunteering for?" asks a young man in a reedy voice.

"To constrain Alabaster," she says, "by strapping him to the table so you know there's no spirit-impersonating shenanigans going on."

"But what about you?" asks his companion. She wears a '50s taffeta dress and pink harlequin sunglasses perched atop her bleached-blonde head. She speaks in a slightly superior way, as if she's in on some kind of joke the rest of them aren't.

"You can tie me up too." Brenda flashes her crooked teeth in a smile. "There must be someone here who knows a thing or two about that."

A few titters but no one volunteers.

Allan looks at Jane. "What about a Girl Guide?" he asks hopefully. "Is there a badge for knots?"

"I'm not a Girl Guide," Jane whispers indignantly.

"Maybe I have the wrong name for it. Brownie? You know, the ones with the cookies."

Jane scrunches her face. "I'm almost fourteen. Even if I *was* a Girl Guide I wouldn't be a Brownie. I'd be a Pathfinder at least."

Brenda clears her throat. "Do we have a volunteer or am I going to have to choose one of you?"

"We can't let her choose," hisses Allan. "She could pick an inside guy."

Ernest points at the spiritualist and Allan nods. He calls out, "We nominate you, Eloise."

"Focus on the wrists and ankles," Allan instructs. "The best knots you got."

She accepts her mission and makes her way to the front of the room, her pointy lace-up boots clicking on the wooden floor.

Brenda lifts herself onto the table and hands Eloise the rope. She lies down on her back and Alabaster joins her, gazing calmly at the ceiling.

The spiritualist sets to work binding and roping Alabaster and Brenda to the table. When she's finished, Brenda invites them to see for themselves: "The bondage no mortal can escape."

Ernest touches Alabaster's hands and feet, inspecting the knotted rope.

"Don't these hurt?" Ernest asks. He wonders if he's channelling Alabaster's discomfort. There's a tightness in his own chest and his muscles ache.

Alabaster doesn't seem to hear. "There are no hoaxes in this room," he announces.

"Whatever happens cannot possibly be orchestrated by human wiles," Brenda adds. "Only by spirits with invisible agencies."

Once they've all had a chance to check the knots, Alabaster tells everyone except the spiritualist to return to their seats.

"Now, open the carpet bag near your feet. Inside you'll find musical instruments. Inspect each one carefully. Do they seem like ordinary instruments to you?"

"They do," Eloise replies happily.

"Any sign of batteries or any other form of mechanical device?"

Eloise shakes her head.

"Please place them by my feet where the spirits will gather. Now, extinguish each candle in this room, for the spirits prefer darkness. When the séance is over, clap and there will be light again. You shall see us here, bound to this table, exactly as you do now."

Eloise blows out the candles one by one. Ernest is aware of his pocket watch ticking. He muffles a cough.

Jane

In the black velvet air, I conjure Dad's face.

I recite details in my head to bring him into focus. Big white teeth. The mischievous way he combed his fingers through his hair around balding men. The summer freckles on his nose. The gold charm of two grappling wrestlers that he wore on a chain around his neck.

"Spirits, are you there?" cry Alabaster and Brenda, their voices echoing off of each other.

The breeze picks up, tugging at my hair and sleeves. I wish we could see if any objects or people were levitating. Will we see the dead softly glowing when they arrive?

I crouch low in my chair and huddle with Ernest, pretending we're weathering something normal, like a storm.

A female voice rises up, murmuring a spell. Ernest wraps his arms around me for extra protection.

The energy shifts. The wind disappears. Ernest releases me and we sit up straight in our seats.

Then—a rapping. Ten sharp staccato beats.

"Contact!" breathes Eloise.

A presence. I can feel it. A gentle weight, as though someone is resting their hands on me. I touch my shoulders but find only collarbones and cold air.

Bells ring and the maracas and tambourine shake and rattle. I blink. The raps quicken, ricocheting off the walls around us. A low moan, not quite human.

Goose pimples break out on my skin. I'm suddenly terrified of the very thing I came here for. Of Dad transformed into a spirit or a ghost. I fight the urge to run.

Dad, are you there?

The raps turn into a light patter. Hands splashing water. Then, a cackle. A toddler's giggle.

The breeze inside the house gathers force. Dad's not here yet but he could be on his way, shimmying through dirt and worms, passing through towns and cities and walls to come to me.

The wind howls in my ears, mingling with the child's babble. If another spirit can show up, why can't Dad?

I reach for Ernest, not sure if he's crying because the ghost kid is Evelyn or because it isn't. A couple of other people in the audience are sobbing too. The demented music approaches and recedes as if the musical instruments were orbiting the room above my head. I squeeze my eyes shut and wait for Dad, summoning him with all my might, light flickering inside my lids.

The raps become slower. Heavier. A dullness to them now. Like bodies thrown around on gymnasium mats.

Is that you, Dad?

He took me to a wrestling practice at the University of Western Ontario once. We sat with his old coach, breathing in air that tasted like stinky feet. The wrestlers wore singlets that didn't cover their nipples and had embarrassing spandex bulges between their legs. I focused on their grimacing mouths and cauliflower ears instead.

I smell the sweaty toes of the wrestlers now. Hear the barefoot squeaks and grunts and panting breath.

I gasp as the tambourine's rattle ascends above my head. A sharp gust of wind in my ear. Or is that a referee's whistle? Could it be Dad this time, grappling there on the mat?

Bodies shifting in time and space. I lean forward and place my hands on the ground, ready to creep through the darkness to Dad.

Eloise's quick clap and I'm thrown back into my chair. The chandelier glows, revealing the haunted house, with Alabaster and Brenda tied up as before.

Brenda's body stiffens and jerks. Her eyeballs roll back. She opens her lips and projects a giant glob of sticky white goo.

Ernest and I scream.

"Ectoplasm!" Eloise cries, face shining.

The room erupts in excited whispers.

Alabaster and Brenda transition to the cabinet portion of the séance. When Brenda asks for another volunteer, my hand rises. I follow Alabaster into his compartment and remember my dream of crawling into the coffin. As I tie him up, a current electrifies my body. I steal glances at his square-jawed face and athletic build, thinking about the ways he does and doesn't resemble my father. When it's Brenda's turn to be tied up, I focus on her Cupid's-bow mouth and my thoughts turn to Annie. Was kissing me in the creek really just for practice? I tighten the knots with all my might.

I close the cabinet doors and return to my seat. The sounds start up again, this time in the light where we can see.

Moans and wails and panting breaths that ricochet off the walls, invading me. A tambourine rattles on the floor before lifting itself into the air. A couple of shakers rise.

A burst of lilac. My father's jogging steps, just ahead of me on the trail.

Allan charges the stage. He pulls open the cabinet doors. Brenda sits on her untied hands and Alabaster tries to hide his bell. Musical instruments crash to the floor.

A brief silence while everyone processes what's happening. Eloise is the first to break it.

"Coward!" she bellows.

"It's not what you think," shouts Alabaster.

I turn to Ernest, frantic. "How did they get out of their bondage?"

All the effort we made to get here. Everything we risked.

We wait for Brenda and Alabaster to assure us that it was the spirits making the ghostly sounds and music, that what we heard and felt in the darkness was true.

I cringe when I think of how my fingers lingered on Alabaster and Brenda's skin. How could I have been taken in by such obvious actors?

Meredith

On their way back to the car, Meredith and Ruth pass a mural of a bear in a field of flowers. He holds a gas mask in his furry paw and stands in radioactive green peonies. Meredith runs her fingers along the wall. Jane would like this neighbourhood too, she decides.

She sees a salon called Jane's Hair. Next door, a used record shop that probably has a Siouxsie Sioux record or two. Meredith takes these reminders of her daughter as indications that they should stay and poke around the area.

"Ready?" asks Ruth, unlocking the car.

Meredith hesitates.

"You hungry? I know we skipped lunch. But there's some tuna fish sandwiches in the cooler. There is the mercury to think of. But the store was out of salmon, so—"

"I want to spend more time here. How about getting some—" Meredith strains her eyes to read a sign. "—Tibetan food."

"Tibetan food?"

Meredith points to the restaurant. "My treat. Then we can take off if we uncover a lead."

Ruth looks at her hopefully. "You feel something?"

Burr

Southwestern Ontario had its own magic. At London's Grand Theatre—built on the site of an old Catholic cemetery—the reflection of the former owner, last seen alive in 1919, sometimes appeared in the backstage mirror.

There were witches who stole animals' souls, leaving the pristine carcasses on the grounds of Princess Elizabeth elementary school. There wasn't any blood on the corpses of the cats, dogs and parakeets, and no signs of broken bones. It was as if they had simply fallen into an eternal sleep.

Even in Burr, locals were willing to suspend their disbelief. Superstitious farmers washed their trucks and sprayers and dried clothes on the line to coax a rain. During droughts, they prayed for the birds to fly low, for the ants to fortify their walls, for spiders to scuttle down their webs, for the sheep to turn toward the wind.

Some farmers castrated and dehorned animals on a waning moon to minimize bleeding. Slaughtered on a waxing moon for juicier meat.

At Oxbow public school, the practice of tornado drills in portable classrooms required magical thinking too. The kids crouched face down in the prefab death traps, the tops of their heads pressing against the thin walls as they covered their necks with their hands. The gym teacher joked about what would actually happen in such an event, the bits of Milligan and Jones and Valentine found mingled with the debris.

Jane

We hang around on the sidewalk after most of the other angry and dejected attendees have gone home.

"I don't get it," I say to Ernest, feeling sick. "There were so many knots."

"Tight ones too," Ernest says. "I triple-checked."

"Are they magicians? Slipping their way out of knots learned in magic school?"

Ernest kicks a rock. "We didn't get to see the 'hands and arms of various sizes appearing and disappearing in plain view' promised in the ad. I was looking forward to that part."

"Me too. And seeing Dad on his birthday."

Allan and Mona saunter up to us. "Sorry to have ruined your experience," he says. "But it had to be done."

"Who are you, anyway?" I ask.

"Allan is a medium in his free time," Mona explains.

His grin fades.

"Psychic," Mona corrects herself. "I always get those two mixed up."

Allan takes off his US Army ball cap. "I'm not a medium or a psychic," he says, addressing the perfectly curved brim and spitting out the terms as if they're covered in cat hair. "I'm a paranormal investigator."

Allan reaches into his pocket and offers us his business card. Underneath the leprechaun-green lettering that spells *Allan*

Duffy Paranormal, a sexy ghost pouts from a coat of arms, hair writhing Medusa-like around her head. Her wrists are in shackles and her breasts burst out of a lace-up bodice.

"Thank you," Ernest says, bowing slightly.

"Does she really need triple-Ds, Allan?" Mona asks, peering over my shoulder at the card. "Men," she says, rolling her eyes.

"Down with the patriarchy," I say, worrying I mispronounced *patriarchy* when she bites her lip. It's one of those words I only come across in Mom's books.

"What about the raps?" Ernest asks Allan. "How did they do that?'

"That's some Fox Sisters, Davenport Brothers crap right there." Allan cracks his knuckles in our ears, replicating the sound. "If they have any talent at all, they can do it with their toe joints too."

"And the thumps?"

"Heels of their feet, probably. How they freed themselves both times is what's stumping me." Allan scratches his head. "They've got to be good at creating rope slack while appearing to be doing nothing."

I remember the froth shooting from Eloise's mouth. "What about the ectoplasm?"

"Cheesecloth. Another classic Victorian trick. You think they'd update things a bit."

"They did have the clap-activated lights," points out Mona.

"What a charade. Discredits the whole field of afterlife professionals..." Allan sighs. "Heading home now? Need a ride?"

"Home's kind of complicated," I tell him.

"That's too bad," Allan says. "You know," he adds after a moment, gesturing to his Walkman-type device, "I'll be analyzing the recordings at my apartment if you want to come."

"Is that what you were doing? Recording?"

"Just some standard EVP stuff," Allan says casually.

"EVP?"

"Electronic Voice Phenomena. Sifting through acoustic anomaly to decipher messages from the dead." Allan crosses his fingers. "Hopefully. This house is *way* off the electromagnetic field meter for paranormal phenomena. As soon as I turned the ghost meter on, the needle went wild."

"So, even though the raps and moans were fake, you believe actual real spirits are here?"

"My ghost meter certainly thinks so."

"How do I know you're not a fake too?"

"There aren't really fakes in the EVP scene. Just the occasional idiot who forgets to remove their camera strap when they take a picture." He laughs. "Then, when the strap falls in front of the lens in a photo, they're convinced they've captured a vortex."

"A vortex?"

"Passageway between worlds. On my bucket list, for sure. *Extremely* rare. So what do you think?"

I turn to Ernest.

"It would be totally free, of course," adds Allan. "Any semi-respectable paranormal investigation is strictly non-profit."

Ernest lifts his shoulders to say it's up to me.

"I guess we could go for a bit," I say.

"Great," Allan says. "Mona, come too. Say, do you guys like sushi?"

"Love it," I reply, even though the only seafood Mom and I ever eat is regular old fish and chips.

Ernest

Ernest had assumed the paranormal investigator would live somewhere modest and subtly spine-tingling. Instead, he and Jane follow the Duffy siblings through a gleaming white lobby with hunks of red plastic masquerading as chairs. The doorman returns an escaped hair into his pompadour. Why does Allan choose to live in such a place and how can he afford it?

There's no soul in this lobby. No history in its walls. Unlike the haunted house, this doesn't seem like a place a spirit would frequent at all.

That's why, Ernest realizes. Paranormal investigators must be like everybody else. They need their downtime too.

They enter the waiting elevator and ascend smoothly to the eighth floor while over the speaker, robotic voices chant above basic synths and drum-machine beats.

When Allan ushers them into his salmon-coloured open-concept abode, Ernest feels as though he's entered some kind of hip movie set. Day of the Dead sugar skulls bare their teeth at him among black and white photographs of seashells and Stonehenge.

Ernest sniffs the air. Vinegar and lemons. Allan presses a couple of buttons on a remote control and a sitar begins to drone over a hand-drummed beat.

There's nowhere to sit other than the dining nook. Ernest leans against a wall and pretends to read an anthology of ancient funerary texts. He tries not to stare when Mona takes a shiny black pouch from her purse and begins to paint Jane's face. As Mona blots Jane's newly crimson lips on a tissue and coats Jane's lashes with a wand, he feels a pang of sadness.

"Girl Guide dropout meets Elvira," Allan says approvingly as he walks by, clutching the bag of takeout sushi. "Did Mona tell you she used to be a professional makeup artist?"

"Whoa, really?" asks Jane.

"Really. Punk and rock 'n' roll bands, mostly."

"Did you ever meet PJ Harvey?" Jane asks. "You look like her."

"I wish. I worked with North American groups, mostly. Anyway," Mona says, packing up her potions and brushes, "that was a lifetime ago."

"Ernest," Allan says. "That's your name, right?"

"Yes," Ernest says.

"All good?"

"He's shy until he gets to know you," Jane explains, talking about him as if he wasn't there.

"Well," Allan says as he gestures for everyone to come to the dining area. "Let's all get to know each other."

Ernest tentatively takes a seat. He's never had sushi before. He's shocked by the rice bundles draped in a rainbow of flesh. He breaks apart his wooden chopsticks and waits for Allan to bring them something to cook the rolls on.

Allan pours soy sauce into four small blue-and-white dishes and blends green Play-Doh into them with his chopstick. "Can't forget the wasabi," he says as he passes them around.

Allan plucks a pale pink slab, dips it into the sauce and places it delicately into his mouth. Swallows. Mona does the same.

Ernest is horrified. "You eat it raw?" he blurts out.

Mona and Allan laugh. "He's funny," Mona says to Jane, pointing at Ernest with her chopsticks.

Jane avoids his eyes.

He decides to do it too. To pop the raw fish in his mouth nonchalantly, as if he's been eating it his whole life. He fumbles with the chopsticks and drops the sushi a couple of times, but on the third try he gets a good grip, gives it a dunk in the sauce and raises it to his lips.

His hand is shaking and the maroon fish jiggles as if it were alive. Ernest wretches involuntarily and clears his throat in an attempt to cover it up. He closes his eyes and slips the mermaid snack in. He chews carefully. "Mmm," he says.

He's surprised it's actually not that bad. He could even grow to like it.

Jane widens her Cleopatra eyes and tentatively prods a sushi roll on her plate.

The ghostly white rolls are more of a challenge. Ernest double-dips them into the sauce to disguise the rubbery texture. Wasabi burns his nostrils, the way he'd imagined it would feel when a bad guy held a chloroform-soaked cloth over someone's face until they passed out in a film noir.

Could Allan be a bad guy? There was something phony about his corporate death-tech shtick. Something... not right. He narrows his eyes as Allan gets up and takes a jewel case out of the tower. "This will really transport you guys to Japan," he says, slipping the CD into his stereo. The music, with its twanging strings, sparse rhythms and undulating male vocals, is gut-wrenchingly sad.

"Jane," Ernest whispers while Allan obsessively adjusts the bass and treble levels, "I have a funny feeling."

Jane plucks a piece of pickled ginger with her chopsticks. She's about to speak when Allan twists his torso to catch Ernest's eye. "Shamisen," he says in a jovial voice, but Ernest suspects he drew out the *shh* on purpose to silence him.

Ernest seizes a striped orange-and-white piece. He chews as the music plays on, the shrimp firm and sweet, the red beads bursting on his tongue. He chews for Jane and for his eternally swimming sister, fishbone necklaces swinging from her neck.

Jane

Allan's condo reminds me of a place I once saw in a mail-order catalogue. At the time, I'd never seen anything like it. The furniture had exotic names with circles and dots over the vowels and almost everything was white or made of pale wood. The kitchen was sparkling clean and on the dining room table were perfectly spaced meatballs on square plates. What I remember most was how bare the surfaces were. There was zero clutter. I wondered who lived there. A stylish monk or a Zen record label exec, probably.

I ripped out the picture and pasted it in a notebook. I decided to move into that Ikea place when I was done hanging out in dive bars. It looked so modern and enlightened. I imagined myself rolling Swedish meatballs between my palms in the kitchen. My friends would come by in the evening to spear them with toothpicks between sips of flaming absinthe. Later, we'd improvise music, plucking the gut strings of my harp and pounding on drum skins. On the empty living room floor, we'd construct a Buddhist rock garden.

Annie made a face when I showed her the glued-in page, back when she was a punk in Converse. She said it looked like yuppie puke and I could do better. Frankly, she was disappointed in me. She was going to squat in Manhattan after we graduated high school and I should come because it was going to be legendary, unless I was too scared of bedbugs and pickpockets and gorgeous geniuses with skin-tight jeans and rehab pasts. I was in awe of her rebel attitude then, but look at her now, and look at me.

Here I am in the condo of my dreams with Ernest by my side, hanging out with a paranormal investigator and his servant of death sister. We're eating sushi with chopsticks and listening to secret ghost recordings from a busted séance hoax. If Annie and I are still best friends and I tell her about this night, will she believe me?

Allan tells us about the origins of EVP over sushi. About an Estonian artist named Friedrich Jürgenson who listened to his own bird recordings and found among the chirps the voices of his dead wife and father calling his name. And about Konstantin Raudive, a Latvian parapsychologist who carried on Jürgenson's work of recording, transcribing and translating messages from the dead.

Allan stage whispers his favourite line: "Here is night, brothers. Here, the birds burn."

"Get this—after *Breakthrough* was published, Raudive switched his focus from recorded voices to animals, most famously Putzi the parakeet, who spoke in the voice of a dead fourteen-year-old girl," Allan says. "That must be about your age, right Jane?"

"Basically."

"Raudive's pioneering EVP research is what he'll be remembered for though," Allan says. "Definitely his strongest work."

Could there be spirits all around us, struggling to be heard? I think of people speaking in tongues on late-night TV. A glitch in the VHS. A snowy screen.

We don't know where our spirits were before we were born. How can we know where they go when we die?

I tell myself not to get my hopes up. Not to be fooled again. EVP isn't necessarily real, just because Allan believes.

"My former wife was a skeptic," Allan says, as if he can read my mind, "of all things paranormal. Then one day, she calls me at work. 'Al,' she says, 'I had this feeling in the bedroom, like there were cobwebs all over my face. Then, a blue baby crawled toward me on the floor.'

"The next morning her breasts were hard. It was the baby's doing. He wanted to suckle from her. She wanted to sell the house.

"'Now calm down a minute,' I told her. 'We just need to find out what he needs to go on his way.' The blue baby opened up during the EVP session. How his mother had died in childbirth. How his father had hastily remarried. Thing is, the baby looked just like his dead mother. The second wife saw red every time she glimpsed his cooing face. In a fit of rage, the stepmom drowned him in the bathtub."

"Kinda big vocabulary for a baby," Mona says, placing a cigarette between her lips and rifling around in her purse for a lighter. "To explain all of this to you."

"The blue baby was dead for a long time, wasn't he?" I jump in. "So maybe he picked up some words from all the people he haunted?"

Allan glares at his sister. "The blue baby was actually over one hundred years old when you take into account his entire post-mortem existence."

Mona watches him carefully. "It's just interesting that ever since I became a thanadoula, you have this resurgent interest in the Other Side. You quit your career in real estate and now you've got a job in death tech and you're dabbling in spirit photography and EVP in your spare time. It's like, even though we're adults now you still have to one-up me. I'm helping people transition peacefully out of this life and instead of feeling happy that I've found my calling, you feel the need to claim you're having deep connections with the ghosts of murdered babies."

"I'd love to hear your stories, Mona. But whenever I ask about your death servant work, you cite patient confidentially."

"But what happened to the dead baby?" I interrupt.

"He was lonely. Could you blame him? We brought him into our bed and my ex-wife nursed him while our five-year-old son slept in the next room. After a few nights of this, the baby crawled into the afterlife."

"She nursed him?" I ask, wondering if the milk from his wife's breasts looked as though it was gobbled by air.

"That, I believe," says Mona. "I've seen mothers clutch their stillborn babies to their chests, as though they thought their milk might revive them."

"Let's play the tapes," Allan says. He turns off the CD and fiddles with his equipment while everyone relocates to the bamboo floor.

"We have to be patient," Allan tells us, his finger poised on the play button. "There could be an important message hidden among hours of static. A single sneeze and you miss it. Or—" He taps his tape player. "—there could be nothing at all."

At first, the recordings sound like white noise and I tell myself, at least I got to hang out with some interesting people, even if they aren't dead yet.

A snippet of sound. I grasp Ernest's hand. But then it's gone and we're back to the static.

Dad would drive me to school when I'd miss the school bus. I channel-surfed the whole way, scanning the airwaves for a rare Hole, Tori Amos or PJ Harvey track among the classic cock rock and annoying ads. I'd usually only find them on the Detroit or Toronto radio stations but there was a lot of hiss and crackle since we didn't live close to either big city. Dad wasn't a fan of static or skipping around and would threaten to put on one of his Roy Orbison, Johnny Cash or Cat Stevens CDs if I didn't settle on a channel, stat.

My dad was the kind of guy who turned the volume down if there was a crescendo and back up whenever the music grew soft. That's how much he wanted to be calm and steady. He kept doing it, even though I told him it was called "dynamics."

Allan stops the tape. "Did you hear that?" he asks, flushed. He rewinds for a second, turns up the volume and presses play.

The tape gasps and struggles. Then, a sinking. An expulsion of air.

"Is this a good idea?" My voice is high and scared.

"If we were in the haunted house I could converse with the spirit in real time," says Allan excitedly. "Still, this is promising."

A gurgle. A submerged scream. Who were we contacting from behind the veil?

"Heeeellloop," growls the spirit, rushing toward us through the tide.

"Hello!" Allan cries, his voice bouncing off the hard surfaces of his condo.

The growl turns to a hiss.

"I heard 'Hell,'" Mona says uneasily.

"What about you, Ernest?" Allan asks. "What did you hear?" Ernest shakes his head.

"Jane?"

I look down at the transparent cassette in Allan's player, the tape pulling from one reel to the other. "Help."

We wait and wait but the voice doesn't come back. If we each heard a different word, does that make it any less real? And what about my father on the wrestling mat earlier? No one mentioned anything like that after the séance. Do we just hear what we want to? I watch my nails tear themselves apart.

I don't need to listen to an EVP recording to know what Dad would say to me now if he could. *Go home. Be with your mother.*

"Let's take a break," Allan says when the tape runs out. "I need a coffee before we get to side B. Anyone else?"

"Black as the heart of a crone please," says Mona.

"So why did you come to Toronto, anyway?" Allan asks me as he puts on the kettle. "Searching for someone on the other side?"

I close my fist to hide the pile of fingernail slivers. "Yeah."

It's time to grab Ernest and get out of here. But Allan doesn't want us to leave.

"You're sure you don't want coffee or tea? I don't get many visitors here," he says. "Just Mona occasionally."

I motion to Ernest that we're leaving. He doesn't notice through his coughing fit.

"We have to go," I tell the siblings, "but thanks for sharing the EVP tapes with us and the sushi."

I glance around the room. Allan's condo isn't as dreamy as when we first arrived. It's obvious to me now that the hanging photos of the stone circle and the beach are just the ones that came with the frames.

"I hope you find your vortex someday."

"I hope you find what you're searching for too," Allan says.

"Hey—" Mona interrupts. "Is Ernest okay?"

Ernest

Ernest had watched everyone carefully while Allan played the tapes. The black box had crackled like a beat-up radio. Underneath, a high-pitched hum, a TV tuned to colour bars. When a voice appeared briefly amidst the static, Jane jumped, Allan's eyes flew open and Mona grabbed his hand. But it had just sounded to Ernest like warped snatches of lyrics and movie dialogue. Like his John Lee Hooker cassette tape after he accidentally left it on the dashboard of his Thunderbird during a heat wave and it partially melted in the sun.

This was what a paranormal investigator lived for? Ernest had sipped from his tiny cup, unimpressed. Allan had forgotten about his hosting duties, so Ernest started topping up his sake himself. The taste was slightly sour but he liked the buoyant way it made him feel.

After a while Allan pressed stop, but the recording device had a life of its own. A cat mewled from the broken radio, desperate, in heat. Then, an onslaught of static and a terrible laughter that floated toward Ernest on a swoosh of wind. He covered his ears but couldn't keep out the ha-ha-ha-has of those childhood gulls, the lapping of the lake.

On his third cup of sake, the air grew wet and his sister swam toward him.

He reached out to touch her and her fins cut him. *What the heck?* He grasped for her.

Let me go. A flap of a tail and she's gone and now he's back in Allan's condo and he knows where the sea went. He coughs and sputters on the bamboo floor. The water is inside him, has been secretly pooling within him for days, drowning him from within. Sea foam dribbles from his mouth.

"Ernest, what's wrong?" Jane's worried face looms over him.

He wants to tell her but his teeth are chattering. He's worried the sea will burst out of him and engulf her too.

The wailing starts quietly and grows louder. Men carry Ernest onto a white-sheeted cot and push him into the elevator. As soon as the doors open, the wheels of his cot are turning and he's flying up the ambulance ramp. Jane races after him under spinning red circles of light.

The men lift Ernest's head and place a plastic mask over his face. A snorkel. He's relieved they understand, the air coming in easier through the water now.

Jane is talking to one of the men, convincing them to let her come.

She's there when they unload him in the parking lot and she's there jogging alongside him as he's pushed down one hallway and then another as his whole world goes under.

Meredith

A waiter beckons Meredith and Ruth to follow him down a long carpet through the restaurant, past empty red tables and chairs edged in gold. He pulls two chairs out and they sit. The Dalai Lama smiles benevolently through a glass frame.

Meredith orders butter tea and momos based on the waiter's suggestions before heading down the stairs to the basement washroom. As she rubs the pink liquid soap into her hands, she examines the way the lines on her palms crisscross and loosen, like unravelling braids. Which line represents longevity? Which line, love?

She wonders if she'd recognize the creases in Jane's palms and the swirls of her fingertips. Are her daughter's nails jagged and her cuticles raggedy, or has she grown out of her nail-biting habit without Meredith noticing?

The hand dryer blasts droplets from her fingers and lifts the cat hair off her shirt. The air blows desert hot. Meredith closes her eyes for a moment. She's dreamed of visiting the pyramids in Egypt too. After she's reunited with Jane, she'll take her there on a mother-daughter trip.

Meredith pushes the door and climbs the stairs. She's about to turn onto the main floor where Ruth waits when she notices a painting tacked up on the wall half a flight further.

A blue demon rides her mule through a sea of blood. She wears a crown of skulls and flaming jewels in her wild red hair.

The goddess should be terrifying, but instead Meredith feels protected under the watch of her three bloodshot eyes.

A sudden grunting makes her jump. For a moment, she wonders if it's the mule in the painting. She listens. No, it's coming from above. She picks up other sounds. The creaking door of a haunted house. A nest of hissing snakes. A sound she imagines a baby dragon would make.

Is she, as in a fairy tale, being led to an enchanted place?

The staircase leads to a room that's bare except for juniper incense smouldering on a side table.

Meredith hears voices. She tilts her head and reaches up on her tiptoes to tug the hanging rainbow of knots. A panel in the ceiling opens and a rope ladder tumbles down.

A vulture flaps across a bright blue square of sky. Meredith grips the ladder and begins her ascent.

Jane

Ernest is shaking in the ambulance and his lips are blue. His eyes blink. Something frightening is unfolding. Something I can't see. Allan thought it might be a fish allergy but Mona disagreed. "Suspected alcohol poisoning or acute pneumonia," she told the emergency operator on the phone.

Their worried faces receded as we pulled away, bisected by the ambulance doors. The séance and the EVP session didn't bring us Dad or Evelyn. And being here made Ernest sick.

I run my fingers along Ernest's face encased in the oxygen mask, his breath hissing in and out.

We hurtle toward the hospital. After that, where will we go? I picture Mom on the side of the road with Dad dead at her feet, the neighbours' headlights merging into a single blinding light.

I deserted her too. Unlike Dad, I chose to. Once I get Ernest out of the hospital, I'll face Mom and what I've done.

I squeeze Ernest's fingers one at a time: *Stay. With. Me.* On the last pinky, I take a deep breath before pressing *Please* into his pale white bed.

Meredith

Meredith raises her head through the opening. A group of people stand on the roof. She counts about thirty. They're curiously quiet for a party. They're not mingling either. They seem to be waiting for something to begin.

Meredith places her hands on the roof and pushes herself up to standing. A few faces turn toward her and she notices handkerchiefs tied over their noses and mouths.

A woman with an asymmetrical haircut and a black cape motions for her to join them. Her dark eyes glitter and her neck is encircled by strands of coral, turquoise and lapis lazuli beads. Compelled, Meredith accepts the invitation and positions herself toward the back of the group.

The air feels as though the oxygen has been sucked out of it, as if everyone is holding their breath. Meredith holds hers too. The air stinks of rotten meat, and when she does inhale, she gags. There must be an abattoir nearby. Funny she didn't notice it earlier. The wind must have picked up, spreading the stench.

The caped woman pulls a red handkerchief from her pocket and gives it to the teenage girl standing beside her. The girl approaches Meredith and ties it gently over the lower half of her face.

"Thank you," Meredith murmurs to her retreating back.

She cranes her neck to get a better view. In the middle of the gathering, a young man blows into a conch shell, trumpet style.

Two men kneel on either side of him. They're wearing plastic ponchos, like the ones they pass out on the Maid of the Mist boat tour at Niagara Falls.

The crowd tenses. Meredith creeps closer, the tiny hairs on the back of her neck bristling. Something is about to happen. The kneeling men raise their arms, revealing hatchets and cleavers.

Meredith sees what's lying on the ground between them. She gasps. The air shimmers for a few seconds before the men let their arms drop. The vultures scream, draping their shadows over the gathering, momentarily blocking the sunlight with outstretched wings.

Were her eyes playing tricks on her? She rubs them, disbelieving.

She looks again. A corpse. A human corpse, lying there on the ground.

Meredith shivers as it's hacked into pieces. Shards of bone and gristle fly from the men's hands. She can't bear to watch. But she also can't look away.

Could it be a real body? The birds think so. They clack their curved yellow beaks as they approach the white cloth. One hops past Meredith, pimply pink skin visible underneath its feathered coat. The vultures lift one leg than the other, stretching their claws into the air.

Meredith has heard of a Tibetan ceremony where the deceased human is offered to vultures, returning it to the air. She'd heard about these ceremonies in a documentary—a sky burial, they'd called it. It was one of those documentaries where a British man in khaki shorts and a white button-down travels to an "exotic" place to marvel at its wonders.

Is this a sky burial?

Meredith fears she may be intruding on something sacred,

like the British man in the documentary, but she can't make herself move.

The chopping ceases and the men remove their handkerchiefs to mop their brows. They joke and laugh with the crowd in a language Meredith doesn't understand.

She draws on what she remembers. "A jovial mood eases the soul into reincarnation," the British narrator had lectured.

Meredith thinks of Henry's sombre funeral. How it hadn't made her feel any better. How the open casket had felt like a strange display. "Sky burials are private ceremonies, and outsiders, and their cameras, rarely allowed," the voice had intoned. The screen had filled with drifting clouds, the actual dismemberment and body-pecking action occurring off-screen.

Meredith's brow crinkles. If the documentary was to be trusted, why had the woman in the cape welcomed her to the ceremony? Was Meredith so marked by grief that the woman could read it on her face and body?

The vultures jump and squawk, twisting their necks as bits of flesh fly through the air. The spinal column emerges from the corpse, whitening as the vultures pick it bare.

"Brilliant," someone breathes into her ear.

Meredith whirls around.

A woman with frizzy hair appraises her from violet-rimmed eyes. "You're from the art world too, I suppose?" the woman asks.

"What does the art world have to do with this?"

The woman gestures and suddenly Meredith is aware of cameras swooping and diving in tandem with the birds' movements, filming everything. How could she have missed them?

The woman watches her. "It's still real," she says, reading Meredith's mind. "Even if it's a performance."

"Real, as in, that's a dead person over there."

She nods.

"How is this allowed?" *Surely, you couldn't stage a sky burial in Toronto with an actual real human body in the name of art, could you?*

"Tsering doesn't ask permission to make art."

"Who... is the body?"

"Tsering's lover."

Meredith expels her breath slowly. The red handkerchief flutters.

"She adopted the hatchlings when he was diagnosed with terminal cancer," the woman continues. "She trained them with dead mammals, small ones at first. Voles, weasels, that sort of thing. Over time she gave them bigger bones to pick."

"And now her partner's," Meredith whispers. She thinks of Henry's body in the dirt, being eaten by worms. It isn't so different, really—sky and earth.

The woman leans in. "Only a few people outside of our art community are notified of Tsering's performances. She's the Damien Hirst of the art scene here. Or more accurately, he's the Tsering of his art world."

Meredith knows who Damien Hirst is. The infamous British artist who suspended a fourteen-foot formaldehyde-pickled tiger shark in a vitrine. Hirst was a star, meaning his brand of shock art was becoming more mainstream. But this is something else. It's not shock, it's love and grief and art all mixed together.

The woman's eyes sparkle. "Isn't it fantastic?"

The vultures take flight, the heavy, hunched bodies growing weightless, the man's remains dispersed between hungry beaks. Meredith follows them with her eyes as they soar, the dead lover swallowed into their feathered bellies, transforming into fat and fuel and shit.

Meredith swallows. "Yes," she says, keeping her eyes on the birds. "It is."

Ernest

Ernest gazes at the pastel-blue walls as the hospital intern removes the IV from his arm. He doesn't want to be a patient again. The blue reminds him of the Easter eggs Mother used to hide. She didn't make it easy, smiling enigmatically when Ernest and his sister begged for hints, not caring if they found them.

Occasionally, Ernest stumbles upon the eggs now, or what remains of them. He dug one out from the grandfather clock with his fingernail when he was investigating why the hands were keeping their own time. As he'd licked for chocolate dust, the tinfoil had crumbled on his tongue.

Jane touches his arm. "The doctor's speaking."

"Is there someone who can take care of you?" asks the man.

"I can take care of myself."

The doctor sighs. "You're stable now, but I'm not discharging you from the hospital unless I'm confident your pneumonia will be managed."

Ernest is relieved by the diagnosis. Glad to have a respectable explanation for his shivering and difficulty breathing. Maybe the pneumonia was partly responsible for his recent visions too.

"I need to know a responsible adult—" The doctor glances at Jane. "—will be in charge of administering the oral antibiotics, making sure you're resting and drinking lots of fluids."

Ernest nods.

"It's important that you're sleeping," the doctor continues as his eyes graze over their dirty clothes, "indoors."

"I have a home," Ernest says. "In Burr."

"You probably haven't heard of it," Jane interjects. "It's near London."

"Oh," says the doctor with interest. "Southwestern Ontario. Pretty area."

"It's okay."

"Wait here. I have to consult with my colleagues and then I'll be right back with some paperwork." The doctor exits and the intern follows, closing the door behind them.

Ernest leans over. "Thanks for offering to take care of me."

"Thanks for not dying," Jane whispers back.

"Is he going to let us go?"

"Where would we go if he did?"

"Do you want to go back?"

"We have to sometime, right?"

The doctor is taking a long time but Ernest doesn't mind. Jane rests her head on his chest and he loosens his hands in her hair. He traces sandcastles on her scalp until everything dims.

Sleep surrounds them, soft and dark as a womb.

Meredith

Tsering gives Meredith a triumphant look before turning her attention back to the birds, cloak flapping behind her like an art-punk vampire.

Meredith descends the rope ladder and stairs in a trance. She finds Ruth in the dining room, peeved.

"I've been waiting for you," she says. "Well, actually I didn't wait to eat, because everything was getting cold, but you know what I mean."

"Sorry," Meredith says, joining her. Her stomach rumbles. She takes a small bite of a beef momo and chews. "I got turned around on the way back from the bathroom."

Ruth gives her a strange look. She takes a deep breath, as if she's trying, with effort, to let it pass.

Meredith's eyes well up. "Thanks for bringing me here, Ruthie."

Her best friend grasps her hands. "Of course."

After Meredith finishes eating, they cross the street to a pay phone to check in with the police. Meredith dials the number on Kyle's card and presses the receiver to her ear.

Jane

Past the square blue shoulders of a policeman, I spot her. Hair brushed, face clean. Momlike. Parent-teacher-meeting-presentable, even.

Except she's extremely anxious. She's biting her lip as she elbows her way through the officers. I tremble. The damage I've done. Her cheekbones jut out of her face as if she's lost weight. Her eyes dart around the room, searching for me.

"Mom!" I shout over chatter coming from the policemen's walkie-talkies. The blood rushes into her cheeks and I'm reminded of the time my parents burst into the clothing store at the mall after they feared they'd lost me forever. I wave my arms. "Over here!"

"Let me see her," she says frantically as she pushes her way to me. "That's my daughter."

Her arms are around me and she's crying and I am too.

"Are you okay?" she whispers.

I nod, breathing her in.

"You sure?" Mom combs the bangs off my forehead with her fingertips.

"Are you okay?" I ask.

"Better now."

"But you're shaking."

"Never mind that." Her mouth moves as if she wants to say more. "C'mon, let's go home," she manages, gripping my hand.

"Before we go, we have to do one thing."

"What's that?

"Take care of Ernest."

"Take care of him?"

"Until he gets better."

"Let's discuss in the car."

"He doesn't like hospitals. I'm not leaving him here."

"Ruth will drop him off at the bus station then."

I pull away. "He has pneumonia."

"If this is about money, I'll pay for his ticket."

"It's not about money."

"What's going on?"

"What do you mean? He's sick—"

"I know he's *sick*," she says, in an awful voice. "I wasn't planning to get into this now, but ... did he ..." She hesitates, her eyes searching my face. "Did he—kidnap you, Jane?"

"It was *my* idea to come here. Why won't you believe me?"

Her eyes move between Ernest and me.

After the policemen finish questioning us and I tell them for the hundredth time I wasn't abducted and that we don't want to press charges, they finally go on their way. When Mom promises to drive Ernest to his follow-up appointment in London, the doctor leaves us alone too.

It's raining again. Ruth is waiting for us near the hospital entrance, holding umbrellas. She stubs out her cigarette with her foot, her face breaking into a grin. She kisses me on each cheek then holds me at arm's length. Her smile fades when Ernest emerges from the doorway behind me.

"Ernest is catching a ride with us," Mom tells her quietly.

Ruth twirls toward her. "What?"

"I don't want to cause any more trouble," Ernest says, shifting his weight.

"It's okay," Mom says to him abruptly, before turning back to her friend. "Ruth, please," she says, eyeing the approaching reporters.

"I'm not letting him in my car."

"Listen, I'm not happy about it either."

I touch Ruth's arm. "I'm not coming without Ernest."

Ruth's quiet for once, her lips pinched and white. We stare at each other until she drops her gaze. I know then I've won.

I share my umbrella with Ernest, holding it high to protect him from the rain. As we follow Ruth to her car, I gaze at the CN Tower in the distance, transmitting radio and television signals all over the city. Toronto is just two and a half hours away. I can come back someday.

"Earth to Jane," Ruth calls from the driver's seat. "Get in."

Ernest and I clamber into the back seat, strapping ourselves in on either side of a plastic gnome.

When the rain stops, the world comes into focus. Out of my window, the sky is blue but I can just see the moon.

PART THREE

The torch of the incendiary looms on the midnight air
and dark forms, knife in hand, prowl near the dwellings
of the sleeping village.

—*London Advertiser*, 1877

Burr

It all started with a baseball, expertly pitched, through the window of Ernest's piano room. It was Andrew who did it, supplying the ball (and later, the bats) from his gym bag.

And it was Andrew's best friends, Jason and Dave, who squatted primly over Ernest's flowerpots, depositing a spiral of shit into each one. After wiping their asses, they gave each other low fives, whooping joyfully.

"Ass-sphincter-says-what?" Jason shouted over the Cypress Hill blaring from the boom box.

"What?" Dave punched the air in time with the rap.

Hyena laughter. "Yo, you fall for it every time!" someone yelled.

"You're a waste of sperm, Dave!"

Dave replied by scream-singing the lyrics to "Insane in the Brain."

Ernest's property was the perfect setting for a tailgate party. They called it a tailgate party even though most were too young to drive and there was only one actual tailgate (belonging to Randy Wayne, who had a penchant for eighth grade girls and had flunked a million grades) to party around.

The kids were surprised they hadn't thought of it earlier. Far enough from town, there would be no one to complain about the noise or call the cops on them. Now that the geezer was gone, they didn't have to worry about him lurking around in his pyjamas, messing up the party atmosphere. Anything that happened (the trampled grass, the litter, the inevitable broken glass) wouldn't matter because he deserved it—and he deserved a whole lot worse too.

Everyone grew drunker as the night wore on, Ernest's overgrown yard providing the illusion of privacy as they groped and stumbled and peed and puked among the swishy weeds and grasses.

Some girls played Truth or Dare, but everyone already knew from past sleepovers and the sorority game who had given a hand job to whom and who hadn't kissed a boy yet, not even closed-mouth, not even once.

They swigged from Bacardi Breezers for courage. "Dare," giggled each girl when it was their turn.

Talk in a British accent for the next three rounds.

Dare.

Get down on all fours like a dog. Attach your belt to your choker necklace as a leash. Jump and lick Jason's face.

Double dare.

Pull out your tampon and hang it from Ernest Leopold's door knocker.

Double dog dare.

Write *Meet me at the bleachers at midnight XO Crystal* underneath the bloody tampon and include Crystal's actual phone number.

Triple dog dare.

Tag the fucker's house.

It was Class President Angela who brought the spray paint, lifted from her sister Althea's room. (Althea had scrawled Hole lyrics in lipstick all over the grade nine Home-Ec walls and was planning, over her resulting suspension, to spray-paint stencils of feminist icons onto buildings that symbolized structural oppression.) Angela and the rest of the Burr Elementary Spy Network lacked Althea's revolutionary bent and were drunk on coolers, so they aimed low: simply trying to hold the nozzles steady and to spell *Pervert, Pedo* and *Get Out* correctly. Even the girls who weren't playing joined in.

When they were finished, they debated whether a quadruple hog triple dog double frog dare was a legitimate challenge and whether you could one-up someone on a triple dog dare at all. It was becoming a bit academic. After a few minutes, they gave up trying to come to a consensus.

Someone turned up the radio. Angela screech-sang to "Zombie" while she and her friends circled the house with arms held out straight. They were too excited to be undead.

They held rocks in their hands. They'd forgotten whose turn it was and they no longer cared. Except for Tracy, whose right wrist hung limply, as if she wanted to let go of her stone. She ran her tongue over her braces as Tiffany whispered in her ear, bracing herself for the role she'd been cast.

They shrieked as the windows shattered, examining the ones that held up, tracing the spiderwebs of cracks.

Did they do it for Jane? Although they'd grown up with her, no one could claim they really *knew* her other than Annie, who was yelling into Andrew's flushed face to stop it, right now, and take her home.

It probably wasn't for any deep reason. They did it because they could. Because it was fun. Because they were mad at their parents. Because they needed to prove themselves. Because they were bored. Because they got dumped on Friday. Because they felt like actors in a bad movie.

They didn't mean to set Ernest's gloomy fortress on fire. Or not initially, anyway.

By the time Angela found a canister of gasoline in Ernest's

garage and poured it along the mansion's perimeter and by the time another kid lit a match, it didn't seem like there was much left to destroy.

The flickering flame in Andrew's hand looked respectful, reverent even, as if he were about to light a votive candle. Andrew hesitated. He realized this could change his life forever. He looked around for someone else as Annie tugged on his arm and begged him to leave.

Crystal emerged from behind the trees, the train of her too-long white dress catching on burrs and soaking up drippings of gasoline. She took Andrew's match. As the cheers rose, she received, for an instant, what she'd wanted. She was a different person without her usual neediness, her face illuminated and almost beautiful. After the crowd counted down from ten, she lobbed the match behind her with an angry cry. Crystal bolted as the mansion burst into flames, not realizing for a few moments she herself was on fire.

Slipping on puke and crumpled beer cans, smoky-eyed and choking, the other kids tried to get away as fast as they could. Andrew ran to the nearest farm to call for help. Try as they might, they couldn't outrun Crystal's desperate shrieks and the stench of her singed hair.

A couple of them stayed. Tracy ran around searching for a water bottle among the empty cans while Annie tried to beat the flames out of Crystal with her bag.

Meredith

Meredith feels like her old self, almost.

But when she applies her lipstick in the mirror, her wild eyes shine back and she's reminded of the wolf from *Little Red Riding Hood* masquerading in Grandma's clothes. The comparison is ridiculous. Little girls are the last thing she feels like eating.

At night, though, she dreams she's hunting. She pursues unseen prey through fields and mud, panting hungrily.

One morning, after the school bus picks up Jane, she heads to Ernest's property, stepping around fresh police tape and rubble and crushed beer cans. It's been ten days since the fire. The blaze photos published in the *London Free Press* haunt her with every step. The serpentine plumes of smoke. The roof on fire, the gingerbread sizzling. Each narrow window a hellish flaming mouth.

She wanders around the near ruins, gazing at the charred turret and the remains of the wooden gables that splinter the blue sky. How could this have happened?

Something like this happened before, of course, over a century ago. Then too, Burr had been a community bound together in hate. There was an attack on a local homestead and a terrible arson that became the subject of books and plays and local legend. No doubt some of the perpetrators last week were descendants of that vigilante mob.

She's begun to like Ernest, despite her reservations. If other townspeople got to know him, surely they would too and then they would forgive her for letting him into her home. Ernest is unfailingly polite and tries, in his odd way, to earn his keep. He resets the arms on the battery-dead clocks in the house and waters the weeds in the backyard. He concocts unconventional snacks out of dusty pantry ingredients. He serves them on a lacquered tray that had belonged to Meredith's grandmother, along with a herring stew for Groucho. The cat is devoted to him and sleeps in the crook of his knees.

Meredith ducks under the tape and approaches the entrance, the paint blistered from the heat but the actual door miraculously intact.

The fire is under investigation. The reconstruction of the house will have to wait for now. The master bedroom has completely collapsed and part of the roof is missing but Meredith hopes the house will be salvageable.

Ernest stays with Meredith and Jane for now. An olive branch for Jane. Pragmatic too. Less chance he'll run away with her daughter again. She'll make sure of that.

She should head home. She's shared some of Henry's clothes with Ernest, including a belt to cinch the trousers with. He accepted them gratefully, not minding they were three sizes too big.

Meredith had thought it would feel wrong to have a man in the house but Ernest is more like an orphan from a storybook. Would her daughter outgrow her fixation with him, like she did her Nancy Drew and Baby-Sitters Club books?

In the meantime, she watches Jane and Ernest carefully when they are together, just in case.

Ernest

When Ernest finds out what has happened to his home, the violence of it penetrates his body and he feels as though he himself has been beaten and set ablaze.

He is terrified he is living among people who hate him. The fact they are kids, many of them Jane's age, makes it worse.

At night, he feels someone pressing on his body, pinning him down. But when he struggles to open his eyes, no one is there. At first, he tries to convince himself it is Evelyn. About to steal his covers and pummel his chest with her stuffed cat with the missing button eye.

But the weight is heavier than she ever was or could ever have been. Groucho sleeps with him, staying by his side through the terrors.

Ernest wants to thank his little friend. He builds him a fortress out of cardboard boxes, using scissors and silver electrical tape. He snips empty toilet paper rolls into decorative towers and surrounds the whole thing with a slippery sardine tin moat. He borrows an X-Acto knife from Meredith to carve gothic arched doorways. He cuts tiny diamonds of magazine ads and glues them into stained-glass windows that he brushes with shellac until they shine.

There are cisterns full of rainwater and a toothpick portcullis and a drawbridge you can operate with a piece of string. He makes toys out of naturally shed chicken feathers and bits of yarn and foil. He dips a calligraphy pen into black ink and writes, *No birds were harmed in the creation of this royal gymnasium*, in a small, flowing script.

Ernest invites Jane to the unveiling and she brings leftover Christmas crackers from last year for them to pop. They pull out the paper crowns and place them on their heads. Groucho doesn't need one, because felines are naturally regal.

The cat sniffs his new kingdom and rubs his cheeks against the castle walls. He batts at the tinfoil dumbbells in his castle gym, his whiskers poking out of the watchtower.

When they try to engage Groucho in some friendly fire, he slings a paw over the parapet and plays leisurely for a few moments before curling up and closing his eyes to nap. They laugh at his laziness, shelling him lovingly with catnip and dried shrimp treats.

When Ernest thinks about the fire and the hateful graffiti, it makes him want to lie uninterrupted for centuries in an unmarked grave. But then he thinks of how much he'd miss Jane and the smell of rain. If only he could become invisible, like that time he disappeared at Meadowbrook. Free of the casket and free of his skeleton, a low-key spirit haunting the land. (In between ghostly visits, he could carry the timbre of Jane's voice in his ear, the way a conch holds the ocean's roar. And when she dies, she could join him.)

He racks his brain. Turning phantom has to do with having tragic unfinished business when you die. Does he still have enough left after their adventure in Toronto? What if he dies and simply passes over to the afterlife as smoothly as can be?

Then Evelyn sing-songs in his ear and he knows he will always be haunted. He tries to imagine his sister if she'd lived. Swapping ice-cream-stained Peter Pan collars for a crocheted shawl. She'd be middle-aged now, almost elderly. Who would she have become?

It's impossible to know. And so he keeps her with him as she was, as he knew her, as a child. Scissors in her hands as she hacked away at his hair, the blades grazing his neck.

He'll just have to survive what happened now, as he had then.

Meredith

A couple weeks after returning to Burr, Meredith visits her bedroom in the woods. It isn't just hers anymore, she discovers. At least one couple had found it and made it their own. Mud and rainwater and bird shit have nailed it too. She shakes off the leaves and twigs before flipping the bedspread. Whoever was here seemed to have left Henry's possessions untouched.

She brings Jane there later that day, after racing ahead to make sure it wasn't otherwise occupied, then running back to show her the way.

She refers to it as her art installation. "What should I do with it now, though?" she asks, catching her breath. "Just leave it?"

Jane takes in her father's bathrobe hung casually from the knob of a tree, the ties Windsor-knotted from branches, clothing folded and stacked into neat columns on the forest floor. She pulls out a piece of liquorice and takes a small bite.

"Well?" Meredith presses, reaching into the Twizzlers package to select a red braid.

"Let the forest take it back."

Meredith is reminded of her Chernobyl fantasies. She savours the artificial sweetness and grins at her daughter, pleased.

Something's off. Meredith can see it in her daughter's face. "What's wrong?" she asks.

Jane stares at the hanging portrait of her father. Her eyes move to the suitcase resting at the foot of the bed, then the family photos clamped to the clothesline strung between two trees. She blinks hard.

"You don't like it?"

"When Dad's things vanished, I didn't know what it meant."

Jane tears what's left of her liquorice into pieces.

The ants drag crumbs of Twizzlers behind them like shiny red cabooses. Meredith's throat constricts. "I should have told you I did it."

"Or not done it at all."

Meredith meets her gaze. "You're right."

Jane takes another piece of liquorice, a glimmer of triumph in her face. She sits gingerly on the bed while she eats it, brushing off some fallen leaves with her palms. When she's done, she reclines. Tentatively, Meredith joins her. Through the canopy, the sun drifts in and out of clouds as Henry's silk ties rustle in the breeze. They rest there together in silence, looking up.

Jane

Annie broke up with Andrew after what happened at Ernest's mansion. Now she says she doesn't know what she saw in him.

"You had a thing for hemp and puka-shell necklaces?" I ask her. "A kink for jock sweat?"

"Ew," she says, giving me a push.

"Beats me," I say, laughing as I careen off the kitchen island.

She digs around her wallet and pulls out a photograph clipped from a photo-booth strip. Andrew is mugging and holding her tight. I can tell Annie spent a lot of time on her hair, wrapping each tendril around her curling iron in an ozone-depleting fog of hairspray. She looks like someone else; like post-punk hurts her ears and she'd never constructed grand plans for us in New York City. Her mouth is open and her eyebrows raised in a teen model mixture of surprise and delight.

"I'm glad you're not that person anymore." I hand the photo back as though it's covered in cooties.

"I am too." She tosses it into the trash.

She's over and we're making cookies. Things were kind of awkward for a while so part of me still holds back, not sure I can trust her.

"Who are you going to transform into the next time you fall for someone and ditch me?"

"You blocked me out," she says, catching my eye. "I didn't choose Andrew over you."

We're going to get through it. We're trying to, anyway.

We press the cookie cutters down and remove the excess dough. We're supposed to be making Halloween cookies but I could only find our Christmas cookie cutters. Scooping dark chocolate sprinkles into our palms, Annie and I look at each other and grin. With a toss of our hands, we turn everything goth. Now there are sooty snowmen and ebony stars and candy canes transformed into Grim Reaper daggers. We shove the raw cookies in the oven as the Creatures shriek and drum from the speakers.

Annie fidgets with her pillbox ring. "Is baking black cookies cute?"

She's already pressuring me to give up my Ouija habit ("Hasbro boards are so commercial") and claims she'd love to cast a hex on Andrew. I'd be content with a banishing spell, personally.

I roll my eyes at her. "We'll get to the real spells soon. Are you worried we're Baby Bats?"

Annie groans. "Yeah, or Mall Goths."

"Weren't you basically sorority bound a few weeks ago?"

"Shut up."

"I bet you still have some Lacoste polos in your closet." I tug on her Victorian collar. "Maybe you're wearing one under that black dress."

"Wouldn't *you* like to find out."

I blush, not sure what she means.

"Your mom is so cool," she says, licking some raw dough off her pinky.

"She is?"

"She's probably a real witch and you don't even know it."

Mom's pointy nails. The robe of my father's she's been draping her body in. The growl from under her door when I tiptoed to the kitchen for a midnight snack.

"What's wrong?"

My mind races. What the hell was that thing in the forest a few months back? What was she doing with Dad's clothes and that bed?

I shudder. Could she be some kind of necromancer? I imagine her kneeling on the bed in his unbuttoned nightshirt, taking thirsty drinks from a goblet with blood-red lips.

Mom's dancing around a bonfire in my imagination now, clad in nothing but a wolf snout, and there are others too, devouring sacrificial lambs and loaves of black bread with their middle-aged hands.

"Nothing."

Ernest spends most of his time in the basement when Annie is over. He pokes his head into the kitchen from time to time to see if she's gone, pretending he just needs a ginger ale refill.

They avoid each other. I'm not used to Annie acting nervous or shy. I guess she's ashamed for being there that night. I would be too, if I were her. She watches him when he's not looking.

We skipped class and went to Deedee's Diner my first day back at school. The other kids stared at me and gossiped, but when I saw Annie looking at me with mixed-up feelings in her face, I knew she still cared.

At the diner, Annie asked me what I saw in him, or in her words, "in that crazy old guy." I felt angry she referred to him that way after what he'd gone through and doubted she'd get it, but I took a deep breath and tried to explain anyway. How he knows about music and carnivals and the way things used to be. How he's lost someone too. How he's not afraid of death.

Annie nodded at that, tapping freshly painted black nails on the Formica counter. "I would totally bone Bela Lugosi," she admitted, "if he wasn't dead." As she hummed the Bauhaus song, I could tell she was mulling over whether or not she could accept Ernest on goth grounds. She's still deciding.

We keep the cookies in the oven until they're black around the edges. They scorch our fingertips as we peel them off the baking sheet and pop them in our mouths, charred chocolate sweetly burning our tongues.

Ernest

Ernest likes living with Jane. He likes their shadows on the pavement. He likes the dandelions that grow in the cracks between their linked arms.

He likes going out for walks while she's at school. He likes worm-tunnelled crab apples. He likes nuthatches and blue tits. He likes the hole in the rowboat. He likes bee stings. He likes the green frog and its loose-banjo-string twang. He likes pond scum. He likes the falling maple leaves. He likes the cold face slap of wind.

He is surprised by all this liking.

After the yellow school bus brings Jane home, he likes cracking open nutshells while they sit side by side on the couch. They like the brain shape of walnuts best (and pretending to be zombies when they eat them). They like Boris Karloff movies. They like Orville Redenbacher's microwave popcorn. They like tender, salty gums.

They like tuning into Detroit radio through the fuzz. They like melting ice cubes in their palms then warming their cold dripping hands by the fire. They like how the blood rushing into their fingers brings them back to feeling.

Sometimes Annie joins them, and when she does, Ernest can tell Jane isn't as into their rituals.

He'll have to return home sometime. He can't stay here forever.

He thinks of another project to lose himself in. He'll reveal it to Jane on Halloween, that sacred day when the veil between the living and the dead thins.

Jane

I thought about being a vampire for Halloween, flourishing a cape to conceal my fanged, bloodstained face. I thought about being Frankenstein's bride, lightning bolts in my hair. I thought about being a ghost. "I take after my father," I could joke.

Then it comes to me: I'll be the dead girl who pulls the ribbon loose.

In art class, I fashion a head out of papier mâché and paint it in my likeness. I make a matching severed neck and brush the top of it red. I stick one end of a green ribbon to the neck with glue.

In Mom's closet, a half-buried turtleneck sweater catches my eye. I pull it partway over my head so my face presses against the loose, shimmery weave. My eyelashes brush the furry strands as I breathe in her smell. The world latticed in Secret and pink angora.

Ernest helps me perch the neck on top of my real head, fastening the sweater to me. I carry the papier mâché head like a clutch. He adjusts his black robe before picking up his cardboard scythe.

"You could have been Bluebeard," I say. "He liked headless chicks."

"Everyone's hiding something in the closet," Ernest deadpans. "Maybe next year."

Mom pushes back her grizzly hood to take a Polaroid of us with his camera before waving goodbye with her claws.

We rush into the darkness. Tonight every house is haunted. Giant animatronic teeth clatter on the dentist's lawn as he passes out toothpaste to disappointed dinosaurs and princesses with torn crinolines. We pass eyeballs skewered on picket fences and severed hands reaching up through neat lawns. Pumpkins hold tiny fires and fingers curl around coffin lids. We pick our way through flickering skulls and sugar-high children dancing in glow-in-the-dark skeleton pyjamas.

Fashion police write up fines to mummies for toilet paper on their shoes and "Wearing white past Labour Day" tickets to ghosts. A ring of white-masked Jasons wield hockey sticks. Angela and her herd of sexy cows amble by in spotted miniskirts and hooves.

"Got Milk?" one of the Jasons yells.

A group of Teenage Mutant Ninja Turtles titters. The cows flick their hair in disdain, causing their bell chokers to jingle. I half expect Crystal to amble up in a jersey suit with swaying udders, then remember what happened and shiver.

Angela points at me, her eyes the green of combat camouflage.

"You're the girl from that *In a Dark, Dark Room and Other Scary Stories* book, right? When you took off with Ernest, I knew you'd lost your mind." She grabs the papier mâché and tosses it into the air. My head goes flying, volleyed from cow to cow.

Ernest jumps and misses.

She turns to him. "I'm guessing you're the one who pulled the ribbon?"

I scowl through Mom's sweater. "Don't you know how the story goes?"

Annie swoops in, intercepting the next pass.

"Here," she says.

I hug the head close to my body and look at her with my real eyes, admiring her furry brown bat suit splattered with congealed ketchup and her pearly white fangs. Did I ever tell her how I used to hide upside down in the closet as a kid, waiting for Mom and Dad to discover me, my arms folded into wings?

Ernest interrupts. "I have a surprise for you," he whispers in my ear. "Follow me."

I grab Annie's fingers and pull her along too.

"Wait, where are we going?"

The sidewalk is slippery with pumpkin guts. I don't let her go. A swarm of zombies dances to "Thriller" and Little Red Riding Hood flashes us a wolfish grin.

"I was handling it," I say as soon as we're out of Angela's earshot, "but thanks anyway."

"Right," Annie says.

"Were they always this bad?"

She kicks a rock lying in our path. "Ask Crystal."

My stomach churns as I imagine her post-fire face. Like her old face but with shiny patches, as if parts were rubbed out with an eraser.

A shadow passes over Ernest's face at the mention of the girl on fire.

"I'm sorry," Annie says miserably, "about what happened to Crystal." She forces herself to meet Ernest's eyes. "And to you."

Ernest's jaw clenches. He continues to lead us to his home. I grip Annie's warm hand and his cold knobby one, feeling the finger bones through his loose skin. We pass broken broomsticks and tiaras, a superhero cape snagged on a picket fence and a treat bag on the side of the gravel road, spilled candies glittering like stolen jewels.

When we arrive at Ernest's property, Annie makes a face. She doesn't want to enter but I pull her with me, ducking under the police tape. We stride past the flickering cat-o'-lanterns to the charred entrance, her wings bumping against my shoulder blades. As we climb the partly fallen-in steps, we cough at the smell of smoke and ash and something worse: burning hair or plastic. A swatch of black silk tied to the doorknob flies in the breeze.

Annie points to where the roof is partly missing. "Is this place going to collapse on us?"

Like at the séance house, the door creaks open, as if of its own accord. A billow of purple laughing smoke envelops us. We enter tentatively, followed by Ernest.

"Before the rise of funeral homes, it was customary for the dead to be received in the front parlour," he says, gesturing to where a coffin lies on a walnut dining table.

When I get closer, I realize the coffin is actually made of painted black shoeboxes. Each one is labelled with a different body part and holes are scissored out for hands to reach inside. We feel around the different compartments.

"Ewww." Annie freezes, her fingers inside the brains box. "What *is* this?"

Ernest points to the sign with his cane.

"No, really. Tell me."

"Steamed cauliflower," Ernest admits.

"Let me guess," I say, squeezing a handful of guts. "Cooked spaghetti?"

He nods and tells us the rest of the ingredients. Skinned grapes for eyeballs. Sliced hot dog for tongue. Corn husk for witches' hair. Sliced carrots for fingers. Dried apricots for monster ears. Assorted dried pasta for bones. Baby carrots for toes. Popcorn kernels for teeth. A peeled tomato for a heart.

My eyes burn as I finger the cold pulp. Where is Dad's heart? Was it inside him when I last saw him? Is it rotting inside his skeleton right now? I squeeze the skinned tomato, letting the red juice dribble over my fingers. Or did they take it out before applying the formaldehyde and makeup? Is it in the freezer at a medical lab? Tossed in some waste receptacle for body parts? Is there a use for a dead heart?

Ernest excuses himself. We slide our backs down the peeling wallpaper, bits of it crumbling in our hair. We sit on the floor and Annie pulls Ernest's tarnished flask from her pocket. "Ta-dah," she says.

"Annie!"

She unscrews the lid and takes a chug. "I'll give it back," she spits.

"Promise?"

She passes it to me. "Promise."

The whisky burns my throat and makes the parlour soft and dreamy. I think about the bar Ernest took me to in Toronto and how I want to take Annie there too. I focus on her furry pointed ears to ground myself. "I've missed you," I blurt out.

"You too, weirdo."

Ernest is gone for a long time. We survey our surroundings from our vantage point slouched against the wall. The missing patches of roof uncover a ceiling of stars. The grandfather clock forever ten p.m., unwound since the fire. The paintings are turned toward the wall and the windows and mirrors are covered in a heavy black fabric.

"Why did he do that?" Annie asks.

"It has to do with the coffin in the parlour," I answer, recalling something Mom told me about old funeral customs. "They did that in the olden days so dead spirits don't get trapped in the mirror, or want to live in the paintings." My voice slurs. "Or wait—was it because the dead person would be horrified to find out they're now a ghost?"

"Maybe it's to prevent the mourners from checking themselves out in all that hot black lace."

We drink until the flask is empty. Annie puts on some of Ernest's records. "I Put a Spell on You," by Screamin' Jay Hawkins, and Bobby Pickett's "Monster Mash." We stagger around the room with our arms outstretched.

I see a girl who resembles me. A miniaturized version with crumpled ringlets and porcelain skin lying on the ground near the piano, her mouth a red stitch. Her doll hair rustles and it freaks me out until I remember the state the house is in. I tell myself it's just the wind coming through—but then her stiff body lifts off the ground as if summoned.

I gasp. She hovers, a foot off the carpet. Her eyelashes flutter.

I spy Ernest in the corner of my eye, holding out his scythe like a wand. I want to ask him how the hell he's doing it but I don't want to break the spell.

Annie hiccups. "What is it?"

Ernest lowers his arm slowly and the doll falls.

I rub my eyes and try to explain. Annie calls me a drunk and asks me when we're going to get out of here.

I spy a shimmery thread glinting from the ceiling. Is it attached to the doll? Did Ernest set this up to delight me and best Drood?

I tell myself it's just a spiderweb. That he really is magical. I don't want to go closer to investigate. I want to believe.

Ernest is sleeping here tonight. He waves goodbye to us from the front porch. The moon is still hiding its fullness behind the clouds.

The candy bag waits on the side of the road. We share a package of sour keys then dump the rest of the contents into my papier mâché head. "Trick or treat," I laugh.

"Treat." Annie pulls down Mom's turtleneck, revealing my face.

It doesn't feel like practice this time. She must have honed her skills with Andrew. Does she taste the big city on me? I run my tongue along her plastic fangs, pretending I'm as experienced as she is. Kiss her lips coated in sugar.

Annie pulls away. "Did you know vampire bats French kiss with mouthfuls of blood to deepen social bonds?"

"Really?"

"Yeah." She bites my lip.

We head toward my house, stopping every few minutes to make out. My body buzzes as her hand moves down my thigh. I hesitate, wonder if this is a punk thing or a drunk Halloween thing.

"Free bleeding?" She teases. "Hardcore."

I take a step backwards. I see red stains on my skirt. Feel a hot trickle down my leg.

"It's okay. I'm a vampire, remember? I'm supposed to like blood."

We stumble up my front porch stairs, shells crunching under our feet.

I look up. My home, shining with raw eggs.

"Dicks," mutters Annie.

Mom is pretending to sleep. Her lamp switches off when we come inside. The box of pads in the bathroom is empty but I don't want to ask Mom if we have more and betray that I've been drinking. A ball of toilet paper in my underwear will have to do for now. I lay a towel on my bed and Annie kisses my curved spine.

Meredith

In the languid late-morning hours of her weekday library shifts, Meredith surreptitiously photocopies tourism articles on the pyramids and rereads Marian Engel's *Bear*. When she discovered the paperback misfiled among straightlaced accounts of mammal psychology and behaviour, she grinned and looked around the room before re-immersing herself in the love story between the Toronto archivist and the farty, chained-up bear.

Peeling away the neat strips of electrical tape that had been strategically placed over the yellowed cover (the prim censorship of head librarian Mrs. Beatty, she suspects), Meredith reveals the heroine in all her bare-chested and wanton-hipped glory. In between duties, she glances at the paperback under her desk, where the ecstatic strawberry blonde on the cover surveys Meredith from within the loose embrace of her furry paramour, beckoning her with a finger.

Meredith closes her eyes every couple of sentences, savouring Engel's tenderness and wit. She understands more than ever Lou's desire to be clawed to death by wildness. By love.

Last week, she forgot the specific smell of Henry's hair. Sometime earlier, the temperature of his skin. She panics as he fades. Each loss of memory is small yet gruesome, a fingernail plucked bleeding from its bed.

Sleeping alone has become normal. When she awakens in the morning, she finds that her limbs have trespassed onto

Henry's side of the mattress. How easy it is for her body to take over his territory in her sleep. How disconcerting.

She'll never get over him. She doesn't want to. She refuses, in fact, to move on. The grief keeps him close. If she can, she'll survive it, carrying the full weight of it through the rest of her life, slung from her shoulders like a pack.

No matter how hard she grieves, she will continue to forget him, bit by bit. Nothing she can do to prevent it. Loss is still loss, no matter how intimately she holds it.

Meredith sleeps fitfully. Underneath her bedroom, Ernest digs for family treasure. He tries to be quiet but she can hear him poking around. Normally, Meredith would bristle at an outsider rooting through their basement.

It's different with Ernest. Perhaps it's his joy when he's found a gem. Super 8 videos of Henry's wrestling bouts. Jane taking her first steps in the snow.

Perhaps it's the uncovered things themselves, which bring to life memories she thought had disappeared forever. The silent black and white footage of Meredith's ancestors that flows together like surrealist poetry. Children giggling noiselessly, dressed in their church finery and an elderly woman stirring bones into broth. Tree limbs furred with lichen and women in cat-eye sunglasses waterskiing in a row. A meatloaf that flies out of the oven then is sliced and plated before an audience of clapping toddler hands.

One day, Ernest discovers Meredith's mint cassette tape of Joni Mitchell's *Hissing of Summer Lawns* among the film reels in the basement. Meredith had been disappointed by the album when it came out, but now she delights in its difficult pleasures, particularly "The Jungle Line" with its snaking synths and warrior drums. She slips the tape into Henry's boom box and sings along to it in the shower, guessing the lyrics and humming over the parts she doesn't know how to fake.

She runs the bar of soap over her skin as the water blasts her body and the glass and mirrors fog. She doesn't care what she sounds like. She sings louder.

Jane

We like chipped black nail polish, pillbox rings and the mall. We like running up the down escalators. We like trying on baby-doll dresses at Le Château. We like our excessively malt-vinegared New York Fries. We like reading aloud our Manchu Wok fortune cookie messages in French.

We like each other's heartbeats. We like flipping through *Spin* by flashlight inside our corduroy-couch-cushion fort.

We like the hot wax drips of candles. We like blasting Hole and the Cramps. We like locking the bedroom door. She likes kissing me and I like kissing her back.

What's happening between us surprised me. I don't know what it means and I'm scared someone will find out. I try to just enjoy the thrill of it. To live in the moment, at last.

Ernest

Ernest shows Jane where the darkroom used to be. She inspects the prints still hanging by clothespins from his parents' curtain rings. The concentric rings of a stump, a dead white rabbit, a kettle full of steam. There's a blur along the edge where Ernest's arm got caught in the frame.

He points out the projector in the hallway, his most recent garage-sale find. She surprises him with reels on her next visit and they set up a screening room in his parlour. They munch on expired After Eight mints.

Ernest tiptoes out from his spot behind the projector to watch Jane's reaction to a reel of her father fly-fishing. He searches Jane's face, finding the lost girl at her father's funeral that he was desperate to befriend. His shadow momentarily superimposes on Henry's, not quite filling his muscular twenty-something frame.

As soon as he realizes what is happening, Ernest crouches so he won't interfere with the projecting rays.

Jane doesn't seem to mind. In fact, she creeps in front of the screen as if in a dream, mimicking her father's actions as best as she can. Their silhouettes overlap and fall apart, one figure coming out of the shadow of the other. Sometimes it is difficult to tell who is on top, who is the figment and who is real.

Jane

Lately, I've been having trouble sleeping. I weave my fingers over my belly button and wonder if plants can hear themselves being eaten. I think up other questions: Is it true that newborn babies believe their hands are just shapes bobbing in front of them? When they die in their cribs, is it from dreams so intense they never wake up? How long until they forget the womb?

As the night crawls, more questions do too. Has Dad's hair grown? Does his skin still smell like candles? How long will it take for the casket to break down, for the plants to poke through the eyeholes, for a train of ants to march up his spine? And when it rains, does his body shift and sigh as though it's alive?

I imagine future archaeologists digging up Dad's bones and putting them back together. An example of an adult *Homo sapiens*, circa 1994. Would they know he was a wrestler? Would they detect courage in his bones? And if they found me buried nearby, could they tell we were related? Could they connect us by our matching square jaws and our crooked second toes?

I pull my bedding over my shoulders. Is Annie under her duvet right now, unable to sleep?

Burr

Winter comes early this year. Salt eats at icy sidewalks, leather boots and paws. Children pummel each other with snowballs on their walk home from school. In their free time, they skate over frozen ponds or lie on their backs, wiping their arms and legs back and forth to make angels.

The older ones hunker together to stay warm, sipping from each other's mickeys or carving love arithmetic into the grey flesh of beech trees. They call their friends on the phone when they get home, their voices transforming into waves of electric energy. Breath travelling between their houses on twisted copper wires when they've run out of things to say.

The adults spray-paint pine trunks to deter Christmas-tree-thieving trespassers. They stockpile their own wood. Light small, contained fires. They make a point to say grace, even if they're only eating microwaved dinners, or leftovers on foldout TV trays.

Their eyes gleam when they hear Ernest's name. They'll never forgive him for running away with one of their children. For bringing infamy back to the town. The fire was his punishment. Crystal's injuries, his fault. When the old sinner dies, it will be his turn to go up in flames.

They ignore the new intimacy between Jane and Annie. Pretend they don't see the lady pigeons building nests together. Goslings diving after two moms. Rams mounting each other when there are ewes in the pen. Male garter snakes emerging from their dens, clad in female perfume. The monarchs who couple gaily underneath their Halloween wings.

At Jane and Meredith's house, the flowers and tomatoes Henry planted wait underground. To burst through the soil for one last bloom.

Soon there will be a shortage of local honey. The Varroa mites have attached to the honeybees and are sucking out their fat. The colonies will eventually begin to recover, but then there will be neonicotinoids, new crop-spraying pesticides, that kill them.

London advances, waves of subdivisions and strip malls taking over pastures and crops. When Ernest dies at the century's turn, his property will be razed for a big box membership grocery store, concrete poured over his wild garden. Shoppers will stroll through the ghost of his Victorian mansion, humming along to piped-in Auto-Tuned singing, filling shopping carts with flats of pop cans and party packs of frozen chicken.

Evelyn

Lake Huron wasn't always a lake. Nine thousand years ago, caribou galloped along its bed, pursued by hunters with obsidian tools.

Evelyn lies on a blanket of zebra mussels. She floats upwards, a drowning in reverse.

Her lungs expel dirt and water. Soap turns to fat, skin loses its pucker. Drifting through phytoplankton and algae blooms and schools of fish.

Look up! In the middle of the blue, a rippling hole of light.

As she nears the surface, her legs begin to kick.

When she breaks through, she's gasping for air in a bathtub with an old man she knows is her brother. He stares at the waves she makes.

He turns the knob of the radio on the ledge, searching for blues.

"It's okay," she whispers through the static. "You can stop saying sorry."

Henry

Henry glides through the walls of his home, bricks and drywall yielding gently. In the living room, he floats over an old man lying on his couch. He's familiar but Henry can't place him. Groucho purrs between the stranger's ankles, kneading the air for milk.

The man's breath is raggedy and his eyes are open as he sleeps. Henry sniffs his spirit the way a dog sniffs another dog's bum to take stock. He doesn't pick up anything ominous, just notes of warmth and gloom, but he still feels uneasy. When the man blinks and dream-sniffs him back, Henry lets him.

I'll haunt you if you mess with my family, the whiff says. Your scapulae will be pressed onto the mat in under thirty seconds. The man curls his knees into his chest.

Henry swims through the wall to visit his wife. He folds the corners of the love scenes in her books while he waits for her dreaming to deepen. When her mouth is parted and her eyelids twitch, he appears, hovering over her as she imagines herself back in the bed in the woods. He slips under the sheets, pressing against her backside. He brushes dream-acorns out of her hair with his fingers. She twists toward him, grasping his face.

Henry's daughter is waiting. She's calling out to him in her sleep. He materializes in his herringbone vest and suitcase. She cries at the sight of him. "I thought you'd died." She notices his suitcase. "Where are you going?"

He's not sure. He doesn't want to go but it's not up to him.
A jay screams. The cracks between the blinds grow brighter.

Notes and Acknowledgements

Thank you to Silas White at Nightwood Editions for believing in this book. Thank you to Emma Skagen, Karlene Nicolajsen and Karine Hack for your editorial brilliance. Thank you to Annie Boyar and Tania Blokhuis for connecting *Burr* with readers. Thank you Angela Yen for this incandescent cover.

Thank you to the University of Toronto's MA in English in the Field of Creative Writing, the Banff Centre for Arts and Creativity, the Sage Hill Writing Experience and Access Copyright Foundation's professional development program for providing uninterrupted time and invaluable consultations during the writing and editing of this book.

Burr wouldn't exist without the generous mentorship of Rosemary Sullivan, Catherine Bush and Gail Jones. I am grateful for your faith and ongoing support.

Thank you to Desert Pets Press, the *White Wall Review*, *Geist* and the *Hart House Review* for publishing early scenes. Thank you to the many friends who offered feedback and writerly support, especially Laura Clarke, Jeremy Hanson-Finger, Catriona Wright, Lauren Kirshner, Emmy Anglin, Ted Nolan, Danielle de Pass, Sarah York, Kate Jenks Landry, Shari Kasman, Ian Sullivan Cant, Phoebe Wang and Marina Hess. Thank you Kate Cayley for your dazzling insights and care with words.

I am grateful for the financial support of the Toronto Arts

Council and the Ontario Arts Council. Thank you to the jurors and publishers who recommended me.

I'm indebted to the musicians whose songs haunt this text, especially graveyard blues pioneers Bessie Smith, Ida Cox, Sid Laney and Spencer Williams.

I appreciate receiving permission to reprint the following Siouxsie and the Banshees lyrics:

El Dia De Los Muertos

Words and Music by Susan Ballion, Peter Clarke and Steven Bailey
Copyright © 1988 Dreamhouse Music
All Rights for Dreamhouse Music Administered by BMG Rights Management (US) LLC
All Rights Reserved Used by Permission
Reprinted by Permission of Hal Leonard LLC

"El Dia De Los Muertos" Written by Steven Severin, Susan Ballion, and Peter Clarke.
Courtesy of Domino Publishing Company Limited.

Visual art also inspired key images and ideas in the novel, namely: Tasman Richardson's public statements about laugh tracks and digital phantasm and his "Life of Death" installation loop, Carrie Marie Schneider's "Dress" video installation and Katie Paterson's "Earth-Moon-Earth (Moonlight Sonata Reflected from the Surface of the Moon)."

Growing up north of London, Ontario, I believed that the nearby village of Birr was named after the spiky plant that clung to the fur of my dog. The deliberately misspelled setting of my novel is a reference to my youthful misunderstanding and a reminder that this is a work of fiction. Burr is a composite of various locales in the area, embellished with Gothic motifs and a great deal of imagination.

Thank you to my elementary teacher, Mr. Marshman, who provided creative writing enrichment and black humour during portable classroom tornado drills so many years ago.

I'm grateful to Dava Spence for telling me about a dog who lovingly dug up his dead feline companion. I miss you and I will never forget you.

Thank you Alicia and Pan Grouios for your kindness and child care. Thank you to my sisters Lisanne and Krissy for your eternal enthusiasm and loyalty. Much love to my fabulous mother Gail who taught me to grab life's bits of joy while I can.

Chris, thank you for supporting me in every way along this journey. Greta and Ramona, you light up my life.

PHOTO CREDIT: ARDEN WRAY

About the Author

Brooke Lockyer holds a BA from Barnard College and an MA in English in the Field of Creative Writing from the University of Toronto. She was the winner of the 2009 Hart House Literary Contest and a co-recipient of both the Peter S. Prescott and the Lenore Marshall Barnard prizes for prose. Her work has been published in *Toronto Life, carte blanche,* the *Hart House Review, White Wall Review* and *Geist.* Born in Southwestern Ontario, she's lived in rural Japan, New York City, Bristol and the Mojave Desert. Lockyer currently resides with her family in Toronto, ON.